THE MAHLER FIVE

Jean Renwick

Published by Jean Renwick
Copyright © 2016 Jean Renwick
Cover design by Sandy Bradley
Printed by CreateSpace
All rights reserved.
ISBN: 978-1-5262-0526-1

DEDICATION

To my late friend,
Anne Suffield for introducing me to
the world of classical music.

CONTENTS

JEAN RENWICK

FIRST MOVEMENT *Trauermarsch*	1
Chapter One – Richard's Story	2
Chapter Two – Georgina's Story	20
Chapter Three – Benjamin's Story	38
Chapter Four – Jeremy's Story	54
Chapter Five – The Girl's Story	66
SECOND MOVEMENT *Stürmisch bewegt*	75
Chapter Six – Richard's Story	76
Chapter Seven – Georgina's Story	87
Chapter Eight – Benjamin's Story	99
Chapter Nine – Jeremy's Story	112
Chapter Ten – The Girl's Story	124
THIRD MOVEMENT *Scherzo*	135
Chapter Eleven – Richard's Story	136
Chapter Twelve – Georgina's Story	148
Chapter Thirteen – Benjamin's Story	158
Chapter Fourteen – Jeremy's Story	171
Chapter Fifteen – The Girl's Story	179

THE MAHLER FIVE

FOURTH MOVEMENT *Adagietto*   189

Chapter Sixteen – Richard's Story   190

Chapter Seventeen – Georgina's Story   197

Chapter Eighteen – Benjamin's Story   205

Chapter Nineteen – Jeremy's Story   218

Chapter Twenty – The Girl's Story   221

FIFTH MOVEMENT *Rondo Finale*   229

Chapter Twenty-One – Richard's Story   230

Chapter Twenty-Two – Georgina's Story   236

Chapter Twenty-Three – Benjamin's Story   246

Chapter Twenty-Four – Jeremy's Story   259

Chapter Twenty-Five – The Girl's Story   269

EXIT   279

Chapter Twenty-Six   280

ABOUT THE AUTHOR   286

FIRST MOVEMENT *Trauermarsch*

Chapter One – Richard's Story

It is the interval. Richard pushes his way through the crowded foyer and spots Georgina standing by the programme kiosk. In summery pink and green, she stands out from the crowd. He is frazzled after his swift walk across town to the concert. No doubt the covert whisky in his office has left him flushed. Georgina, his poised, totally in control wife, looks him up and down and he awaits the inevitable protest and reminder of the consequences of booze after his heart scare last year. Instead she greets him distractedly with a public peck on the cheek. He has seen that distant look increasingly of late. Not tonight's problem though. Once the deal is over, he will root out what bugs her.

He follows her into the auditorium where people are resuming their seats. 'Good first half? Ravel?'

She nods but adds no qualification.

'After the concert I'll walk you back to your car.' He knows she would be perfectly safe alone but it is the least he could do.

'No need. Have you forgotten? Mark's back for his dental appointment tomorrow. He's in town tonight with friends and is meeting me after the concert for a lift home.' He notes the irritation in her voice. 'Will you come straight home or go back to the office?' Her question sounds innocent but he knows she disapproves of his working long hours again. Is her irritation due to that or because of Mark?

'I just need to tie up loose ends for tomorrow.' Instead of the expected bollocking, Georgina nods slowly, for once accepting.

It will give him a chance to listen again to the voice-mail message that he picked up after his meeting earlier. What was that all about? He had not recognised the woman's voice yet it seemed vaguely familiar.

'It's time to meet. I'll call again,' the woman said firmly.

Who was she? He tries to push the memory to one side. Too much else going on for now.

Still over-heated, Richard slumps deeper into the seat beside his wife. His head full of the day's negotiations, he struggles to remember tonight's programme. In answer, a summoning trumpet announces the funeral march of Mahler's Fifth Symphony. His eyes sweep the orchestra, full-on with all eight double basses and a massive contingent of brass. Gloomily he considers the next five movements, his stomach clenched right up to the back of his throat.

Not Mahler, not tonight. And the Adagietto; just what I don't need.

*

I thought my head would explode. We'd been sitting in that airless room since eight. Not even the chance for a break at lunch-time.

'We need to keep going, Rich,' said Mulligan. 'Shall we send out for sandwiches?' It was more of an imperative than a question. Typical of the man, giving orders in my board room. I wanted to punch him. And not just because of the sandwiches.

We ate and kept going, all bloody afternoon and into the early evening. The discussions, as we diplomatically called them, went over the same ground. Neither he nor I were prepared to shift position, not on the financial side nor on the proposed structure, even though we both recognised that one of us would have to cede ground eventually.

I refused to look my two associates in the eye as Mulligan's lot interrogated our figures and projections. Tom and Jason aren't handling the pressure. After all, they realise the extent of the shit we're in. Opposite sat Mulligan and his advisors. Body language revealed their confidence in what they view as a done deal. What possible leverage do I have to protect our position? If I don't find inspiration tonight, tomorrow we start the marathon when both legal teams close in to finalise the transaction.

By seven fifteen I was desperately in need of space to think and I realised that Georgina would be settling into her seat with the concert about to begin. We'd booked it months ago along with loads of others. Couldn't remember the programme but whatever, the concerts are always good and music would clear my head. Could I make the second half?

It was a pretty shallow ploy, however everyone in the room knew what happened last summer and I was past caring what any of them thought, least of all Mulligan.

'Sorry folks, I'm going to have to call it a day for now. After last year's spot of bother, I just have to pace myself otherwise I'll get a bollocking from the wife.' My laugh sounded weak even to me.

Why did I always underplay my collapse? 'A spot of bother.' Christ, I thought I'd bought it. I've never experienced fear like that. Swimming in and out of consciousness. I knew I was lying in an ambulance and the couple of paramedics tending me certainly weren't cracking jokes. Given that history, Mulligan was unlikely to push back. All the same, I didn't want him to find out that I was sliding off to hear a symphony concert just as things were hotting up. He didn't challenge.

'Sure,' he smiled. 'You carry on.'

*

One thing is certain: my business cannot survive as it stands, whereas Mulligan's consultancy seems to tick over nicely. I can appreciate the benefit of size and my North West client base would make a great fit with his Basingstoke set-up. A merger with any other competitor would be just about acceptable, but not with Mulligan.

He's always been a devious bastard and he won't be playing a straight game this time either.

I just need Saddlethwaite council to hold off terminating our contract, even for a few weeks, at least until after due diligence and the deal is signed. This is when I need to call in my favour from Ian Black. As Saddlethwaite's contracts director, he can make or break a successful deal. If I'm going down, I'm determined that it's for the best price possible. Ian owes me this at least.

Last summer Georgina totally pissed me off with her initial resistance to my plan.

'For heaven's sake, it's only two nights and Amberley Castle is a top hotel. Georgina, you know Saddlethwaite is one of our biggest clients.'

She looked at me across the kitchen and flung her arms wide in frustrated acceptance.

'OK. It's important to keep that creep on-side, but a whole weekend, Richard?'

Of course, in the event, she handled everything superbly and never once patronised either the client or his somewhat tarty companion, certainly not his wife, even though conversation in the candle-lit dining room was hard work. She didn't even wince when the female complained with a giggle over breakfast that the peacocks had kept her awake half the night. As a matter of course, I ensured both parties' tracks were covered; nothing traceable back to me or Ian.

*

Looking at Tony Mulligan across the board table, I reflected on the past we shared. My memory of childhood probably didn't chime with his. I didn't always think him devious. The game-changer occurred the time he came back to mine for tea after a school trip to the Lakes. My father quizzed me in the kitchen when I came to fetch the sandwiches. Where did the boy live, what did his father do? I quite liked Tony then. He made me laugh and took risks when I wanted to but usually chickened out.

I replied enthusiastically. 'He lives down the Hobbins. He's got loads of brothers and sisters. It's really mad there. I think Mr Mulligan is caretaker or something at St Joseph's.'

My father sniffed. 'Mmm. Look, Richard, you've just moved up school and from now on, everything counts. Of course, you'll work hard but it takes more than that. Mixing with the right sort is just as important. That lad'll pull you down; I've seen that sort before.'

I shrugged, not wishing to enter into dangerous territory, and turned, plate in hand, to see Tony standing in the doorway, his look one of confusion and anger. My mother, unaware of the incident, tried valiantly to sustain conversation over the tea table, not understanding why two glum eleven year-old boys gave monosyllabic responses to her enquiries about what we'd seen of Lake Windermere.

The cut-off was immediate and tacitly understood by both of us. Weirdly, we managed to get through the next years at the same school without ever speaking to each other. It was later that our paths again converged.

While reading Geography up at Durham, I worked the long holidays at Bill Edwards' traffic management consultancy. Creating new road links and resolving traffic flow were becoming big business and could be the direction for my future career. I was pissed off to find Tony Mulligan already working there. He'd gone in on the ground floor straight from school and Bill had spotted him as a bright local lad to be encouraged. We both avoided more contact than necessary and Bill never noticed our mutual reserve.

*

After the remains of our lunch were cleared, Mulligan leant into the board table, his fingers tumbling a Mont Blanc ball-point. He was flanked by his Young Turk of a finance director, who scarcely concealed his contempt for our figures, and his PA, an attractive girl in her twenties. She had a particularly direct gaze behind her specs though she scarcely spoke. Her pink and purple dress was hardly appropriate for a business meeting. I wondered if Mulligan was shagging her.

He was about to make his final offer. I knew it was time to face reality but I couldn't forget our interwoven past that had driven years of conflict between us.

After graduation, with Bill Edwards' recommendation, I secured the job at Conningsbury's in London.

On my very first day I was devastated to recognise the voice at the other end of the office.

'So, you've finally made it down to London, Rich,' said Mulligan as he walked towards me, smirking in the knowledge that I loathed my name truncated.

'What took you so long? While you've been up in Durham getting fancy letters after your name, I've been working my arse off down here at the coal face.' First day. A brawl was not the way to start. I gave a non-committal shrug.

'Don't worry mate, you'll catch up eventually. The money here's good too,' he threw at me, aware full well that graduates started on a pittance.

Good consultancies were relatively few so it wasn't really surprising that we'd both ended up in London at Conningsbury's around the same time. We drank with the same crowd after work, even once dated the same girl. Or more correctly, I won her off him. Over the years we grated on each other beyond normal competitiveness: the disagreements in planning meetings about whose traffic solution was better; who was up with the latest technology.

Then came the time when the prick undermined me in a client meeting. It led to my removal from the scheme. When Mulligan was promoted to head the bid for the Winchester project, I raged inside, especially as I'd done the spade-work to get onto the bloody pitch list in the first place. And then I was forced to work under him to put the proposal together. Christ Almighty. To top it all, it was my scheme which won the project that Mulligan would head up. Except that Mulligan didn't. Suddenly he buggered off to set up his own business down the road, at the same time poaching some of Conningsbury's top people. He didn't approach me, though. No surprise there. Until now.

Some years later I received a call from Bill Edwards. I was horrified to hear that he was suffering from advanced prostate cancer.

His voice was amazingly strong.

'Will you come back up north, Richard? I need someone to work alongside me while I can still manage it, then if you're happy with things, I'd like to work out a deal so you could keep the business going. It'd be a shame to see it fall away and it'd add a bit more to my Susan's pension.'

A return to the North West to join a thriving consultancy was a no-brainer. However, by this time, I was married to Georgina with two kids. I knew she would regret leaving London and the cultural buzz of the capital. I was persuasive and made it clear that without this move, my career path would be restricted. It left her little option other than to support me and within a few months we'd come up north with young Jeremy and Mark. By selling our tiny home in Palmers Green, we could afford a much bigger property on the edge of the mill towns.

The business was strong, clients seemed to like me and stuck with me, even after Bill's death. It was at that time when there was a shed-load of work coming in from developers with new housing schemes and government-backed inner-city regeneration, all needing traffic assessments, planning applications. They were the good times, before the economy took a dive. Local authorities first became cautious and now their massive cuts have stopped all future activity. The economists claim it will all come good again but I can't afford to wait until then.

*

Richard's eyes take in the austere white panelling of the concert hall, renowned for its outstanding acoustics. Even the softest violin can be heard from the topmost seats and whenever the orchestra performs at full tilt, it just blows him away. He tries to block out the events of the day, to lose himself in the Mahler. Music helps him cope with dark times, always has done. He adjusts his rimless glasses and regards the conductor's profile as the stocky figure on the podium leans over the orchestra, the thrust of his baton exhorting onwards each section in turn.

Most of these musicians have played together for years, Richard contemplates. *They trust each other. That's why they're so good. Can I trust my own team, even those who have been with me for years? Not sure.*

Suddenly the whole orchestra flies into a maelstrom of discord. Richard feels his body respond as the racing strings mount an attack on the rampant timpani and brass. Gradually the chaos descends into an alert sounded by trumpets and horns. The warning returns his thoughts to the mystery call to his mobile.

Why didn't she leave a name? The number had been blocked.

His eyes rest on the lead trumpet, exposed to the critique of the audience. His skin tingles to that lone, distant call, urging the troops on, a call against the odds that resonates with his own predicament.

*

It's been bloody hard to 'rally the troops' over the last few years, especially when having to let people go. *Let people go*: God, I loathe that expression. It presupposes that people want to leave and the employer is simply allowing it. In reality it's a balance between doing what's best for the company, identifying who will cope with redundancy least badly, and who will take you to tribunal if you get it wrong.

Mahler wouldn't have coped with today's management of 'human capital'. As a top conductor, he had high standards and demanded that everyone met them. It can't have been easy for him. In those days Europe bristled with anti-Semitism. So many people plotted against him. Amazing he had the emotional energy left to compose with all that back-biting, a complicated marriage and serious health problems. At least I don't have to contend with an unfaithful wife on top of a crumbling business and an iffy heart.

*

The first movement surges forwards like a small boat running before lashing winds, under threat but just still afloat. Richard breathes deeply, his thoughts tossing around in his head, struggling for a way to outrun the storm. He has the uneasy feeling that Mulligan is holding something in reserve. Trouble is, he cannot think what it might be. Desperately weary, he loosens his tie and feels Georgina's eyes on him again. To Richard's ears, the distant call from the solo trumpet insists: *Keep going, just keep going.*

*

Fundamentally, Mulligan wants to be top dog, insisting on fifty-one per cent to my forty-nine. No way.

Over the last twenty-five years, Mulligan has thickened out and this afternoon, seated across the table, he leant his paunch against the table and smiled.

'Well Rich, we can present the deal to staff and the outside world as a merger, with both of us joint MDs.'

I hesitated. Anyone with GCSE Business Studies knows that such an arrangement never succeeds but, given the circumstances, what was my option other than to accept? One thing's certain, though, I'll make damn sure that it only works just long enough for me to get something new going, under the radar. Then I'm off.

*

Georgina shifts in her seat, the movement releasing a hint of her Hermes perfume, the *Calèche* she has worn all the years he has known her. He glances down at his wife's neatly crossed legs. The slim skirt of her dress has ridden up to reveal long elegant limbs. Despite his tension, he takes pleasure that the sight can still interest him.

The music washes over Richard as his thoughts return to the deal. What could Mulligan have over him that might force him out before he had the chance to assemble his own exit plan? Richard's empty and stressed stomach churns audibly in a quiet passage as he contemplates his uncertain future. Out of the corner of his eye he sees Georgina turn her head to look at him.

The wind section lilts into a folk-like air reminiscent of a village celebration set among the green valleys of Mahler's Austria.

*

On my tenth birthday, Mum walked into my bedroom and handed me an LP.

'Sorry I didn't have time to wrap it. I remembered you enjoyed that concert the school took you to last year, so I asked Miss Jenkinson what they played and managed to get it in Woolworths.'

I recalled the unexpected emotion at my first concert, watching the conductor sweep his orchestra through the sound pictures of Beethoven's *Pastoral Symphony*. I admired his power of command in directing such talented players in the creation of glorious music.

'You can play it when your Dad's out.'

'Thanks Mum, that's fantastic.' I hugged her though felt slightly uneasy at the implied deceit towards Dad. He thought anything arty was for Nancy-boys.

It's a generation thing. Compared with Dad, I'm much closer to my two boys, though I feel Jeremy has drawn away from me in recent years. As for Mark, he's going through a difficult phase, really difficult phase. Both lads have enjoyed a far better way of life than I ever did; partly I suppose, because my business did well up to now. To be honest though, we couldn't have managed without the in-laws chipping in on more than one occasion. Initially I resisted taking their money but Georgina convinced me that for the sake of the boys' future, we should accept.

Thank God Jeremy will finish uni in the next couple of months. Money is going to be tight, whichever way the deal goes. As for Mark, I don't want to think what universities will be charging by the time he finishes his A levels. It's not that I've been stupid with money, quite the contrary; perhaps I got that from Dad. It's just that now there's nothing put by.

Moving to Greystones wiped out any spare cash. Worth it though. It's in a better area and we've loads more space. The first time we viewed it, Georgina loved its Edwardian grace. She came alive in a way I'd not seen since we left Palmers Green.

'This is so pseudo,' she said, looking round the mock country kitchen. 'It's crying out for an Aga, like Maman and Papa have. It would be so cosy. And wouldn't it be lovely to open out into the garden with a conservatory?'

Even with financial help from the in-laws, it had cost a fortune to modernise the kitchen and add that conservatory. Despite that, I get a real kick when guests walk into the room and are dead impressed. Beyond that, though, it's the family's favourite place to be. Georgina loves working in there, especially after I overcame my instinct for economy and agreed to the installation of her Aga. Home from work, I sit at the large scrubbed table, facing out into the garden, checking stuff on my iPad, preferably with a glass of wine to hand, until Georgina has tea on the table, though she calls it 'supper'. It's best though when Jeremy and Mark are home during the holidays. I'd questioned buying a bigger place at a time when the boys would probably move away, but these days friends are seeing their kids return after uni with no chance of getting jobs, and stay on for years. On balance, I'd quite like that, still having the boys with us. Nowadays Georgina and I don't have that much to talk about.

*

The conductor urges on the players through thunderous chords reminiscent of suspense movies from the thirties.

The wind players point their instruments high for impact, just as Mahler dictated. Richard's eyes move to the violins and he marvels at their physical stamina in these high energy sections of the piece. He seeks out Benjamin, sitting among the second violins, his gaze fixed on the score, occasionally glancing up to the conductor, not hesitating as the woman sharing his desk leans across him to turn a page.

*

Just over a year ago, as Georgina and I drove home from town after yet another brilliant concert, she made a suggestion.

'Why don't we sponsor a player? We go to most of their concerts and I would love to get to know the people of the orchestra.'

I knew how much she missed her music since moving north and her piano playing had never resumed, as she had hoped, once the boys were less dependent on her.

'By supporting the orchestra we would be invited to lots of private things.'

Certainly, our name in every programme as sponsors of a player would do no harm to my reputation in the area. It would be good to get closer to the orchestra and Georgina complains that I have no real interests beyond work.

When the orchestra management proposed Benjamin, we liked him immediately. One of the *tutti* second violins, he was a pleasant, thoughtful sort of guy, someone with depth.

'You must meet Jeremy, our elder boy,' I said to Benjamin at one of the get-to-knows during intervals in the Green Room. 'He's at Birmingham doing music and plays the violin too. He would love any guidance you could give him.'

In time the violinist became a frequent visitor to the house, first as tutor to Jeremy during the vacation and then, during term time, as partner to Georgina at her parents' baby grand in the drawing room. Perhaps he has helped her regain her past confidence. Certainly, Georgina would have been pleased that I invited him and a couple of his mates to play at her surprise fiftieth birthday party last weekend.

Despite my own misgivings for Jeremy's ambitions for a life of music, I appreciated Benjamin's interest in the boy's future. Although I couldn't see it would be much of a career, Georgina made me promise to keep such thoughts to myself.

If things go tits up tomorrow, I'm afraid Benjamin would be one of the first casualties. We simply wouldn't have money to spare for sponsorship. It would be cringingly embarrassing to explain, even though it wouldn't impact on him directly. Georgina would be mortified. It would be so public, having our names removed from future programmes, and she revels in being invited to the sponsors' private receptions. As for the cost of tickets, I can't imagine that we could still afford as many concerts in future. I'm told that you get a brilliant face-on view of the conductor from the cheap seats in the choir but here is where I want to sit. Year after year, we've had the same seats on the right ledge, close to the stage, overlooking the orchestra, with a view of the conductor side on. From here I can look back into the auditorium, spot people I recognise. Often people have mentioned seeing me at a recent concert. It's good to be seen. A seat in the choir? No way.

*

Richard adjusts his glasses and lets his eyes rove the audience seated in the first circle and the opposite ledge, seeking a familiar face to nod to discreetly. His gaze rests briefly on the senior partner of the city's top law firm and the men exchange discreet nods.

*

I wonder how many of the local business mafia will still be interested if the practice goes under? That's the least of my worries, if the deal doesn't go through. The knock-on effect would be catastrophic. I've no idea how I'd manage to keep up the monthly payments to Hardy & Hardy, or even to keep them secret.

*

He longs to move his legs, conscious that his fidgets irritate Georgina. He marvels at how she can sit so passively, her hands folded in her lap. She always appears calm and accepting yet he wonders if that is really the case. God, if she knew the truth, and not just about the business.

As the first movement draws to a gentle close, Mahler's tension relaxes into the soft chords of the strings. Richard relishes the final notes of the muted trumpet and the resentful flute. He crosses his legs, turns to give Georgina a reassuring smile and is startled to see her eyes abrim with tears.

Chapter Two – Georgina's Story

Not the best music for tonight, Georgina sighs, sensing Richard's tension beside her. She loves Mahler's Fifth but these funereal tones will only deepen her husband's despondency. Worse, this music feeds the fear that has swamped her since Jeremy's earlier voice message. Was the call linked to his sudden departure Sunday morning?

Unwillingly, she looks down on the man seated amidst the second violins.

I've been so utterly stupid. Totally naïve. I'll never forgive him for what he's done to our family.

Her mood is reinforced by the darkness of the music which contrasts sharply with the severe whiteness of the auditorium.

She compels her attention back to the growing swell of the first movement. She yearns for gentle strings to soothe her but already she anticipates the jarring undertones of the next passage.

The ranks of musicians dip and sway in response to Mahler's score, their concentration unwavering as they count bars, even in repose. The trumpets reverberate, offering hope before the mood is dragged downwards by the French horns. As the music sidles into a slow lilt, Georgina longs to rock gently in time. At home, playing her music to fill the house, she sways to the rhythm as she moves from room to room. Here, among two thousand concertgoers, convention dictates a silent, emotionless response. Not that this will be the case, she fears. At least one idiot will cough during the quiet of the *Adagietto*, breaking the enchantment of the moment.

'It's a trade-off,' she frequently reminds Richard to still his bristling irritation. 'Either you listen with headphones alone in your armchair or you put up with the coughs and rustles of a live audience and share the exhilaration.' Watching musicians perform remains one of the true joys in her life. She longs to be part of them, though she recognises her own skills are far inferior to these players'.

She marvels at how Mahler's music generates such an elemental consciousness. Her womb aches with the stirred emotion. Not that she would ever disclose this most intimate of sensations, and now not even to Benjamin.

Georgina appreciates that Richard longs to fidget. He never removes his jacket at a concert, even on a warm evening. Tonight he is still flushed from hurrying to make the second half.

Why the hell do you insist on keeping your tie and jacket on in this day and age? And I bet the red face comes from drinking before you left the office. She rages internally along with the storming music. The doctor has warned him to take things more slowly. Some hope. With the merger of his business so advanced, she is amazed that he made the concert at all, though she knows from bitter experience that, under pressure, her husband needs music to soothe his tension.

*

Soon after meeting Richard, I discovered we shared a love of classical music, a passion instilled into me by my piano-playing mother. Then, as now, it isn't everyone's taste and I was happy to discover someone like-minded. From the start, I was always happy to queue with him for stand-by tickets at the Royal Festival Hall. After the concerts, still high as kites, we would discuss the performance, drinking wine until late. In time I dug beneath his northern reserve and discovered a good-humoured man, with enough ambition to add spice to our life together. Hardly a *coup de foudre* but maybe by then that wasn't what I sought.

Later, through our married life, I saw how music calmed Richard when the pressure of work made him unbearable to live with. The brooding anger, born out of frustration. I hadn't seen that coming in our early days.

I remember the time he clashed with Mulligan at Conningsbury's. We'd travelled out to my parents' holiday cottage, close to where Maman grew up in Normandy. With two young boys and money tight, Saint-

Pierre-sur-Dives had become a welcome bolthole, even though holidays together could be stressful. Papa always had little jobs for us, that is Richard, to do during our stay.

Conningsbury's had just won the major bid that Richard had worked on for months, but instead of relaxing, he spent most evenings immersed in some biography, a scotch at his side, playing Beethoven symphonies so loudly he woke the children. He wouldn't discuss what was troubling him and only later did one of his colleagues disclose that Mulligan had commandeered the leadership of the project.

Perhaps it was that early exposure which generated Jeremy's awareness of classical music. Both Richard and I gladly observed his growing interest, stimulated by violin lessons at prep school, both lessons and fees funded by my parents. During his time at boarding school, we worried that his music had become an obsession. He didn't have friends outside the school orchestra and, home for holidays, he withdrew into himself, not interested in making many friends locally. As his talent grew, we supported his decision to read music at university but I felt that deep inside there was something wrong. I decided to meet privately with the music teacher who had encouraged Jeremy over the years.

We met one spring afternoon in a village teashop sufficiently distant from the school not to be frequented by pupils. I explained my private concerns and added:

'Most teenagers go through a difficult stage, but there's something going on which I don't understand. I worry that when Jeremy is home for holidays he clashes with his father. Maybe that's normal between fathers and sons. I just can't get through to him anymore and he's withdrawing from everyone.' I paused, then ventured, 'Is he being bullied?'

My listener, suited conventionally and looking more like a teacher of economics than music, sat without comment. He carefully poured himself a second cup of tea and stirred in the sugar slowly and thoughtfully. I waited, slightly irked that he hadn't offered to pour for me. He sipped from the cup held in both hands, peered at me over the rim, and asked gently, 'Are you quite sure you haven't worked out already what's worrying Jeremy?'

The master talked of his decades working with teenage boys, of how the experience had provided him with an instinct for underlying issues. I suppressed my irritation at his arrogance.

'What I'm about to say wouldn't meet the approval of my politically correct colleagues. Sometimes such withdrawal is due to bullying but also it can be acute home-sickness, fear of failure or,' he ended gently, 'latent homosexuality.' I felt a coldness wash down my back despite the sun streaming through the window of the café. Absolutely not. Not my boy. Not Richard's son. Just because he liked classical music there was nothing soft about the boy. He played rugby, for God's sake. Out of the question.

I thanked the master for his honesty whilst doubting the ethics of his frankness; his headmaster would have disciplined him for such comments. I drove home on autopilot, searching my memory and thought of the gay men I mixed with or had known. None of them displayed the camp stereotypes portrayed by the media. Derek and John were the landlords at the pub near my parents, and though everyone knew they were gay, you'd never have guessed it. They were two very ordinary blokes, welcome members of the cricket team, part of village life. And there was Paul, who I met in the early eighties when we both worked at a French importers in London. I'd fancied him straight away but girls in the office had a quiet word, explaining why I was wasting my time. None of these men appeared anything other than hetero. So how would I realise if Jeremy were gay or not?

The thought of the torment Jeremy might be suffering made my heart ache. Memories of my own teenage emotions replayed vividly in my head. Over the years, I'd fallen in love with various unsuitable men – and I was straight. Imagine all of that if you were gay.

How the hell would Richard react? He loathes gays of both genders. Would he feel otherwise if it were his own son? I imagined the scenes as Richard raged and I defended. No chance. I'd no alternative but to keep this quiet.

For the rest of Jeremy's school days and since he went to Birmingham, I have never spoken of it. Perhaps I hoped that mixing with girls at the university might open other possibilities to him. Eventually I had to admit that I was kidding myself to expect him to turn straight, as if it were an illness from which he might recover. Each time he returned home I walked on eggshells as Richard probed his social life, evidently expecting his son to follow in his footsteps as a 'bit of a guy'. Instead, Jeremy immersed himself in music and Richard barely hid his frustration that he couldn't understand his son, and his fear that, as a musician, the boy would 'never amount to much'.

*

The woman behind Georgina coughs for the second time and slowly unzips her handbag, fearful of making a sound. She rummages for a blister pack of cough sweets and holds it in her hand, waiting for a loud passage before bursting the lozenge through the foil membrane. She stifles a further cough, sucking audibly on the sweet, and noisily re-zips her bag. Georgina sits tense throughout the protracted operation, screaming inwardly: *If you have a cough, sort the bloody sweet before the music starts. And leave your wretched bag unzipped!*

*

Despite everything that followed, I will never forget the first time I met Benjamin. As Richard and I entered the Green Room an hour before the concert was due to start, my eyes went straight to the figure in white tie and tails. He turned to be introduced and I was struck by the candid gaze. I felt his dark eyes flick over me, then Richard. He smiled and shook hands with a confident touch. As Richard fell into his usual friendly but persistent interrogation, a manner that encourages newcomers to relax and probably reveal more than they would wish, I was free to appraise the violinist. Around thirty? Just under six foot in height and wiry in build. As he responded to Richard's enquiries, I watched him run his fingers through soft brown hair which refused to behave. Embarrassingly, I wanted to touch that hair, so much like my Jeremy's unruly mane.

From the conversation, I gathered that Benjamin was born in Vienna of an Austrian father and English mother and moved to the UK as a child.

'How interesting.' I entered the conversation. 'I'm a hybrid too, but the other way round. My mother is French and my father English. I'd be fascinated to talk another time about growing up with two different cultures.' He smiled and nodded politely. I felt foolish. What a gauche thing to say at a first meeting.

Thereafter, Richard and I arranged to meet him regularly either for a pre-concert drink in the Green Room or for a late supper in a nearby restaurant when we would critique the performance and all three of us would slowly come down from the adrenalin buzz of the concert. I loved to discuss the nuances of the music, especially if a piano soloist had featured.

*

The strings race through the passage evocative of a Russian film score. Reluctantly Georgina watches Benjamin as he flexes into the bowing, his hair falling forwards unrestrained. So unlike when he talks with her and the talented long fingers of his left hand unconsciously comb the fringe from his eyes. Those dark brown eyes. Damn those eyes.

The music thrills her, creating a spasm of ecstasy as it leaps, but then comes that warning trumpet, the crescendo giving way to menacing horns.

*

It was the start of the Easter vacation. Jeremy joined us at the concert and during the interval met Benjamin for the first time. After deciding to sponsor a player within the orchestra, our preference had been for a rank and file violinist. We both recognised that Jeremy would never make concert soloist and, by sponsoring Benjamin, we wanted to show how much we valued the contribution of the *tutti* players.

That evening Benjamin offered to coach Jeremy when home from university. True to his word, a few days later he came over to Greystones and, as they practised together, they developed a good chemistry. After all, he was only around ten years older than our son.

During their second session Jeremy suggested I should brush up on my piano playing and join them with something easy to begin with. I was unsure. Maman had taught me piano, along with most of the children in our village, and had been saddened when my marriage and motherhood curtailed what she believed could have been a successful amateur career. I didn't share her view. My playing had deteriorated so much since those heady days of winning music awards when my mother bored her friends with my modest success. The prospect of revealing my weakness to a professional musician made me uncomfortable.

Benjamin stepped in.

'Perhaps you could spend the next few days practising when you've time, so you're up to speed when I next come over?' he suggested.

When I didn't respond, he added, 'Please, Georgina, it would be good fun.' To hear him speak my name sparked a frisson of pleasure. I gave in, ostensibly with reluctance. Inside, my anticipation quivered. I've always feared that place beyond my comfort zone. Perhaps now was the time to face up to the challenge.

As our trio playing progressed, I was amused to recognise my growing fondness for Benjamin, especially when he encouraged Jeremy through difficult passages. I'd also forgotten the fun of creating music with others. After our sessions, all three of us were on a high.

Soon after Jeremy returned to Birmingham for the summer term, Benjamin called and offered to come over to the house to accompany my piano playing. Was I right to agree? Richard had been encouraging when I told him of the joint music sessions. Lately, however, he had become increasingly distracted so I wasn't sure if he was pleased or indifferent. I told myself that it would be perfectly in order to spend a couple of hours with Benjamin, gradually re-building confidence in my playing.

During our first session, I sensed a growing tension between the two of us. Not unpleasant, more disturbing. As he leant over the keyboard to indicate on the score where the emphasis should lie, I breathed in his smell and instinctively felt a dull pain, deep inside me, almost a longing, which frightened me. Even when I'd wanted Richard to make love, I hadn't experienced this physical ache. Initially I pushed the feelings aside. After all, I was a married woman some twenty years his senior. But, to my shame, I enjoyed this disturbing feeling, one that I could hold secret within. What's more, it aroused new longings beyond the purely sensual.

I wasn't alone in feeling an electric current between us. Benjamin had spoken little as we played and then after only an hour he said, 'Really sorry, I'm not feeling brilliant. I shall have to get back and we're in rehearsal this afternoon, so I'm afraid ...' His voice fell away and brusquely he left.

After he left I sat at my piano. My thoughts whirled.

Probably for the best. All getting a bit intense. I probably embarrass him. A middle-aged woman getting the hots for a toy-boy. God, this is excruciatingly awful. What would Jeremy say?

I couldn't stop thinking about him and that night I lay beside Richard, the ache driving away thoughts of sleep. The next morning my nerves were taut. Overcoming my apprehension, I phoned Benjamin, ostensibly to check he was OK.

'Are you feeling better? I was worried about you yesterday.' Before he had a chance to speak, I rushed on. 'Because if you are, we could pick up where we left off. I practised yesterday afternoon and I'd really like to get it right. I'll do a spot of lunch if you've time this morning?' This was where he'd politely decline and I'd go red, mortified.

'Why not,' he responded. 'Let's try to crack that Schumann, shall we?'

*

Looking back to that day, quite simply, I seduced him. The lunch was already prepared, a bottle of Chablis chilled and waiting. I chose a light summer dress in a pale blue that was kind to my skin and set off my hair. Perhaps not wearing a bra had been a tad sluttish?

We started again on the Schumann but I found it difficult to concentrate. Benjamin was visibly tense.

'Look, this isn't coming together for me,' I said. 'Shall we break for something to eat? Perhaps a glass of wine will help.' He grinned and followed me into the kitchen.

'It won't take a minute to get things together,' I said as I moved around my kitchen, conscious of his eyes following me. I was glad the rattan blinds in the conservatory were filtering the harsh sunshine, creating a soft diffused light as I set the plates and food onto the scrubbed wood table.

'Would you mind fetching the wine from the fridge? Here's a corkscrew.' He pushed himself away from the wall where he'd been leaning, and ambled towards me. As I passed him the corkscrew, our fingers touched and I felt that bounding ache rising up through my body into my throat.

Oh God. Stop shaking. As he took the wine from the fridge, I turned and leant against the table to control my trembling hands. I sensed him step behind me and with fingers icy from the chilled bottle, he traced a line down the side of my neck. A shiver convulsed my whole body and I drew a sharp breath – fear, ecstasy, both. He leant forwards and cupped my breasts, his cold hands soaking through the thin cotton, the while pressing his hardness against me.

*

As the summer term continued, I told myself it was purely a physical thing, desperately trying to justify the sex which had now replaced the music. I wasn't really betraying Richard. I still loved him in the way that couples love each other after nearly twenty-five years of marriage. I lived the fantastic highs of enjoying a lover, but I also endured the sickening panic of being discovered. I couldn't stop myself. And life had to go on. A hideous yet delicious deception as Benjamin visited the house each week, ostensibly for music. With new fabrics and colour, my study was transformed into our special place where we explored each other's bodies and minds.

As the long vacation approached, I knew that with both boys back home it would be difficult for me to be alone with Benjamin. In any case he was due to spend a month in Austria with family. Oma, his grandmother was very ill. Our last time together that summer was particularly poignant. He had phoned the previous day to say Oma was close to death and he needed to travel to Vienna quickly.

When he arrived at Greystones, I held him close, as much for his evident sadness for the coming loss of his grandmother as for my own needs.

I felt strange unease as we lay close, yet separate, after our lovemaking. Perhaps, in that moment of heightened sensitivity, what followed should not have triggered the inevitable. But it did.

*

All the doubt and guilt I was carrying surfaced to choke the breath out of me as later I dealt with Richard's heart attack. And yes, it was cowardly to use Richard as the excuse to end our affair but it was such a relief when Benjamin's mobile rang out unanswered wherever he was in Vienna. Leaving that blunt message was totally out of order but I was terrified he might challenge my resolve.

I knew that I couldn't avoid seeing Benjamin. We were bound to meet at the start of the new season. Somehow I manoeuvred to avoid face-to-face contact in the Green Room. I couldn't stand the pretence of polite conversation with Richard quizzing Benjamin on our musical progress.

At the beginning of the autumn term, Jeremy announced that he'd invited Benjamin to go down to Birmingham to hear other orchestras on his non-performing weekends. I'd been mildly surprised then remembered that Benjamin's parents lived in the Midlands, so he would see them too. Irrationally, I felt jealous.

*

It was last Friday, the day before my fiftieth birthday, when Jeremy finally confided in me. He had managed to grab a few days free of revising for his finals to help me celebrate. We sat alone in the sunlit garden, Richard at work, our younger son, Mark out and about.

'Mum, there's something I need to tell you,' he began. My mind raced. This was it. I'd rehearsed this moment so many times. I would listen and show no anxiety, just loving support. I sat rigid, somewhat ashamed at my conceit that he was confiding in me alone. Pride before a fall.

'You knew I wasn't happy at school. Not in the last few years.' I nodded. 'I didn't want to tell you and Dad, but things were not good for me.'

'I wondered if you were being bullied?' I suggested, trying to soften what he was about to reveal.

'Yes, in a way. But not the usual bullying.'

My heart sank. What other sort of bullying was there?

'Mum, I'm gay.'

This was my cue to reassure him, reach over and hold his hand, tell him that all would work out for the best. But my instinctive reaction shocked me. I froze. I froze with panic at all it would mean: weird men doing things to my child; camp boyfriends; AIDS; the reaction of my parents, young Mark, and Richard. Oh God, Richard.

He took my silence as encouragement to continue.

'It took ages to realise how I felt. At first I kept it to myself and then I became friendly with someone from my year and stuff just happened.' I nodded as though I understood, when patently I had no idea what 'stuff' was.

He continued. I wanted to weep when he told me of his dread of bullying, not from the homophobes at the school, rather from predatory bi-sexual older boys. He spared me the details but it was no wonder he had withdrawn into his music.

'Mum, it was awful, but then I went to Birmingham and it was like a fresh start.' Exactly what I'd hoped. His face lightened. 'And then, last year you introduced me to Benny. I had no idea that he was gay too. We just clicked. Music, life, stuff on every level. We just knew that we had something together.'

My head shrieked like the Schoenberg music I loathe. My breathing became tight. I rose from my chair and turned away from him, seeking strength from the green calm of the garden. I strove to hide my shock but I couldn't breathe.

'Knowing how much you and Dad like him, made it easier for me. He knew I hadn't come out and told me that was OK too. Most people aren't aware that he's gay either. Actually, I think he screwed around with quite a few girls at college before he discovered where his real sexuality lay.'

Screwed around with girls. The phrase resounded in my head. Desperately I tried to regain my composure, controlling my breathing as best I could. I fell into my long rehearsed role, kneeling beside him, hugging him as his tears of relief fell onto my shoulder. I stared hard up at the trees, willing my glazed eyes not to spill over, seeing only disaster ahead. I whispered words of encouragement into his ear, but suggested that we waited a while until we told his father. He nodded with relief.

With the concentration of a drunk intent on crossing the room without staggering, I walked back into the house. As I mounted the stairs, tears escaped and coursed down my cheeks. Too late I spotted Mark who had emerged onto the landing from his bedroom, a room that over-looked the garden where Jeremy and I had talked. His face was impassive, even witnessing my evident distress. He turned back. In the refuge of my bathroom, I ran the taps and sobbed.

Tomorrow would be my 'surprise' birthday party.

*

This morning I was tidying the kitchen as Mark finished a late breakfast. He'd stayed on after the weekend party for tomorrow's ongoing session with the local orthodontist. Belatedly I switched on my mobile which signalled a missed call. *Jeremy*. I held the phone to my ear. His recorded voice first sounded tight then descended into angry sobs.

'I have to see you. I'm coming home tonight but won't get there until late. I want you to stay up for me. I need to talk after Dad has gone to bed. We've got to sort this out.'

The aggression in his voice had startled me. I didn't respond. I was frightened. Had Mark heard his brother's voice? His eyes remained intent on the tablet before him.

I looked out of my kitchen window to the fields, still freshly green before the weariness of high summer. My instinct was to duck tonight's concert, but I'd promised to take Mark into town this evening to meet his friends then bring him home after the performance. If I backed out, Mark would read it as disapproval of his friends (true) and I'd face a day of silent aggression. I really need to have it out with Mark. What is wrong between us? What scares me, though, is what might emerge. I fear that during last half-term, he found out about me and Benjamin. How should I handle it? Do I confront him and risk him telling Richard? Or do I just leave it to fester beneath the surface for ever and a day?

Did Mark say anything about it to Jeremy after the party? Something spooked him to make him leave so suddenly and in such a strange mood early on Sunday?

*

The first movement draws to its close. The horns sound distant in the dying moments and the strings soften like falling mist. Georgina stares hatred down onto the player who returns her look without expression. Then, conscious of Richard's gaze, her eyes fill.

Chapter Three – Benjamin's Story

The welcoming applause stimulates adrenalin as Benjamin threads his way between the desks to regain his seat on the platform. This time he is prepared and deliberately averts his eyes from the balcony ledge where Georgina sat throughout the first half of the concert, the chair beside her empty. Although he suspected she might well attend the concert, even without Richard, that first view of her had unsettled him.

Her intrusion on his concentration is an irritation. He feels anger re-surface. Anger at her silence in response to Sunday's text demanding an answer. He stands fussing over the position of the music stand, trying to block out the possible meaning of the text from Jeremy, received just before the concert started.

*

One of the lads in the back of the car whistled appreciatively as I drew up outside the hotel early Saturday evening, but I wasn't at all surprised. Local stone, country-house chic written all over it, just what Richard would choose for Georgie's birthday bash. Christ knows why I agreed to pull together a quartet. Small choice though. They are my sponsors and he who pays the piper … In any case, all four of us needed the extra cash in hand. So, there I was, dancing to his tune. At least I got to call which music we played and had Richard's agreement that the guests would sit and listen to us before the meal. I don't play musical 'wallpaper'.

Surely Georgie guessed that there'd be some celebration for her fiftieth. Maybe having some sixty friends and family along would be the surprise. But she wouldn't be expecting me to be there. I anticipated the look on her face the moment she spotted me. I'd seen that look so often when we were together 'in public'. There'd be that momentary shared look then the veil of deception would descend and she would continue as though there was nothing more between us than a shared love of music.

The hotel manager showed us where to perform.

'Right guys, we're to play at this end of the dining room. Richard's notes stipulate that the party will move into here from the drinks reception at one fifteen on the dot, so let's get sorted before the guest of honour arrives.'

As I looked towards the door, Jeremy, pink-faced and self-conscious in a suit, strode across the room towards me. Inwardly I groaned and I readied myself.

'Hi! Isn't this fantastic? Mum has absolutely no idea what we've planned. She'll be so thrilled to see you all.' I steered the guy away from the other players, scared that he would touch me while we talked. It would have taken only five seconds for Ludo, our cellist, to pick up on any signs of intimacy.

'Will I be able to see you afterwards? I'm only up for this weekend. I've exams on Tuesday morning.' I was shaking my head when the cheers from next door indicated the arrival of Georgie and Richard.

'Oh yeah, cool, Mum and Dad have arrived.' Jeremy turned from me, squeezed my arm and headed towards the reception party. I glanced around. Shit, did anyone see that? Fortunately not, but Christ …

For the next forty-five minutes precisely, according to Richard's schedule, we hung around, tuned up and got ready to do our stuff. I became increasingly edgy, imagining Georgie looking radiant, wafting her way around the guests next door. I always hate the waiting, especially when you're trapped in one spot. I was desperate for a beer.

Finally, the guests made their way into the dining room, Richard and Georgie following. I didn't look at her. I wasn't sure how she'd react on seeing me. I avoided eye contact with Jeremy but I was chastened by the smirk from Mark as our eyes locked.

Our music was delayed further as Richard rose to his feet. I sighed heavily. Not speeches now. I just wanted to get playing and then away.

'Friends and family, you're all very welcome in sharing with me, Jeremy and Mark this celebration of

Georgina's special birthday. Don't worry though, it's not speech time yet. I won't embarrass Georgina until after we've eaten and she's mellowed on the Chablis. First though, there's something I'm sure you'll all enjoy. As you're well aware, music means a great deal to us both and I especially wanted to celebrate Georgina's birthday with some of her favourite pieces played by our friends from the orchestra, led by violinist, Benjamin Kellner, who over the last year has become very close to our family.'

Close? He had no idea how close. Now it was time for his paid piper to perform. I couldn't bring myself to address Georgie before so many people, remembering to call her Georgina, so with a swift nod, we were straight into a cheerful piece of Mozart. We ended on her favourite, part of Rachmaninov's First String Quartet. Not the most humalong piece for a party but I knew it meant a lot to her.

Afterwards, as we took our bow, the applause sounded warmer than just polite. As guests started on the first course, Georgie, ever the well-mannered, walked over to thank us. She looked stunning in a silk dress of emerald green.

'You were all wonderful, thank you so much. It was such a lovely surprise and the Rachmaninov was a delight.' She shook hands with the others but bent towards me and brushed my cheek with courteous lips. I stirred inside, feeling her nearness and the warmth of her body, smelling her perfume. I wanted to touch her but kept myself in check. I drew back, smiling, to wish her Happy Birthday, then went cold. Her unsmiling eyes were pure ice. *What the fuck?* Suddenly the charade was over and she turned smoothly away. We packed up and left.

The moorland flew past unremarked and as I drove the guys into town, I analysed those last few moments. Was it a mask to hide our relationship? No, there was undisguised hatred in her look. Why?

*

Benjamin flicks back his tails and sits down. He nods at the grey-haired woman settling to his left, his companion for the next seventy-two minutes.

The leader completes the orchestra tuning. Benjamin wills himself not to look up to the ledge again but, as his eyes follow the conductor through the string section towards the podium, he cannot avoid seeing Richard, now seated beside Georgie. The conductor raises his baton and Benjamin's eyes lower to the score before him.

The opening trumpet lets fly and the might of the orchestra soars around Benjamin, drawing the shuddering music into the sonorous beat of Mahler's funeral march. Then he is off and away as the violins swing into the lilting theme. His body sways into the bowing, the pre-performance tension easing. Around him, fellow players sit deep in concentration, each intent on crafting music. Joyous, stirring, soothing, heart-breaking. All to touch the soul.

*

For me, emotion is as much a part of music as breathing is to life. I don't understand why some people are embarrassed to weep at music. Oma wept all the time.

She cried the first time she showed me, her only grandson, how to hold her violin and to draw the bow across the strings to create a sound. I suppose much of her favourite music reminded her of childhood in Austria. She and her sister had been among the lucky ones. If they hadn't been smuggled into Switzerland, both Oma and Tante Gabi would have ended up in the same camp as their parents, and died beside them. Much to weep about.

A couple of years later, I stood there, six years old, surrounded by the grown-ups in my grandmother's overstuffed parlour. Oma was again in tears and held onto the arm of my father. They spoke in their mother tongue, at that time my mother tongue.

'Why do you have to move to England? You have such a good job here in Vienna. You were born here, your children were born here. German is their first language and even Rachel speaks German well now. They will struggle in an English school.'

'Mutti, you have to understand. Vienna is a wonderful city and will always be my home, but now it's Rachel's turn.' Pappi slipped his arm around my mother's shoulders. 'Her mother needs support now she's a widow. My sister is close by to help you, and now Rachel needs to be near her mother too.'

The argument continued in the lilting Viennese German I had grown up with. Oma just didn't understand why her son would leave culturally cosmopolitan Vienna and take his family to live in the industrial heart of England. As for me, at that age I had complete trust in Pappi and any trepidation I felt was eclipsed by excitement at the prospect of an adventure. After all,

England wasn't totally unknown. Every past visit to Granny Attwood was a memory of being massively spoilt.

'I've found a good job teaching German at the top private school in the Midlands. They've agreed to take Benjamin and Karen at special staff rates. It'll give them a better future.' Oma's disdainful look expressed all she felt about the British public school system. She bent down to me.

'Promise me, Benjamin, you won't forget your violin. Or me.'

I reached out to hug her but somehow, even at six years old, I hesitated to crush this delicate old lady. Instead I took her hands in mine and, with a gesture beyond my years, I held them to my cheek then kissed them.

'You see,' Oma turned triumphantly to my father. 'He is Viennese born and bred.'

How could I ever forget that small, sharp-featured woman? It was Oma who made me believe I could create music.

Once in England, Granny Attwood took up where Oma left off. After she lost Grandad in his mid-fifties, she played her records all the time to fill the gap he left and she loved her music right up to the day she died. For housework, she chose Gustav Mahler.

'Listen to the music, Benjamin.' She swayed around the room, her arms and duster raised as in a folk dance. I was embarrassed at first, especially when I saw her eyes moisten.

'Can't you see the country people dancing to this? In a minute the sun will go in and there'll be an almighty storm, you wait.' The jolly music gave way to thunderous chords. 'There,' she said with a triumphant grin and she resumed her polishing, vigorously applying her duster along with the powerful beat.

'It's best to hear it live though,' she always told me, so she would take me on the bus that wound its way through the Black Country to hear the concerts at Birmingham Town Hall. At first its tall soot-blackened columns were scary but, with the years, the imposing façade came to represent afternoons when we could lose ourselves in the popular classics. I loved the imperialism of Tchaikovsky's *1812 Overture*, the unrestrained physicality of Strauss's waltzes at the New Year concert. I was enthralled. I wanted to make that music, to be part of that perfectly functioning creature, moving as one, the orchestra.

*

Twenty minutes before tonight's concert started, I switched on my mobile for a quick check while I changed into my 'uniform' for the concert. As I fumbled with the white tie, my phone bleeped and I picked up a text that Jeremy must have sent while we were in final rehearsal.

Must see you in foyer after concert. Urgent. J. At first I thought to ignore it but it nagged at me. Why was Jeremy up north and not doing exams in Birmingham? Just as we received the call to the stage, I replied *OK* before switching off my phone.

It was the first contact from Jeremy since his needy outpouring late after his mother's party. He was upset we couldn't see each other on Sunday before he headed back to Birmingham. Between Jeremy's high emotion and Georgie's icy turn-off, that's clinched it for me. I'm out of here. It's all way too complicated. But how the fuck do I extricate myself without screwing up the job?

*

What a contrast to those early days when I came to know Richard and Georgie.

She was strikingly attractive and her Anglo-French background intrigued me. I needed to learn more about this confident yet diffident woman. Her relationship with her husband was difficult to read.

'Barenboim's recording has to be the best,' Richard said, leaning earnestly across the restaurant table. I caught the look in Georgina's eye as she sat opposite me, fork in hand poised over her post-concert risotto. She recognised that he was out of his depth. I quite liked Richard, but he could be such a prick sometimes. Not for me to argue back, though. After all, he'd just shelled out a load of dosh to sponsor my chair, so keeping him sweet was high priority.

'You could be right,' I said, looking vaguely around the half-empty restaurant to indicate my lack of conviction. 'However, the Solti version takes some beating too.' I can't resist coming back at him. I shouldn't, but it is my territory after all. She said nothing, didn't challenge, even though she had far more knowledge of music than he.

'Georgina, your piano playing.' I changed the subject. 'I understand you reached quite a high level at one stage. Why don't you take it up again?'

'She's far too busy for that now,' Richard replied on her behalf. 'She's into so many charity committees and there's her beloved music appreciation group to fill the gap. Besides, I need her to help entertain my clients.' Georgina raised her eyebrows.

'For the moment I've quite a lot on.' Georgina looked me full in the eye. 'But what will the future bring?' I warmed to her. Brava, if she meant it. Or was it just bravado?

*

I so didn't want to be doing this. Somehow, sitting on the stage surrounded by other players in white tie and tails feels right. Dressed like a penguin, walking through the crowds in the foyer to get to the Green Room? Not the attention I enjoy.

Small talk was the last thing I needed that evening. Pappi had flown out to be with Oma earlier in the day. I'd wanted to join him in Vienna, as much to support him as to see Oma. I couldn't bear to think of her in hospital. He reassured me that I'd have time to go over to see her in the coming weeks. The cancer had only just been diagnosed. But I wanted to see her, to tell her how much I loved her, how I owed my life of music to her.

Despite the crowd in the Green Room, I immediately spotted the son standing with Richard and Georgina. He had her green eyes and a floppy version of her brown wavy hair.

'So, how's the violin going?' I asked after we were introduced, immediately regretting such a dumb question.

Jeremy smiled back, his face resembling his mother's even more. 'Great.' Nobody else spoke, no doubt also thinking what an inane question.

'Benjamin, I'd love to hear how you got this far. Like, playing with such a brilliant orchestra.' It embarrassed me to realise that the boy was in awe of me, for Christ's sake. Poor sod. I remember feeling like that once. Everyone else seemed to have achieved the success I craved. If only he knew the reality. I felt sorry for him, and there was something about him that appealed. Maybe those eyes again.

'You're home for a few weeks so why don't we meet up? I'd be happy to give you some advice, hear you play and all that.'

What did I just say? I couldn't believe I'd offered to tutor him. Time was precious enough and I needed to earn as much as possible out of working hours. What a prat.

'Benjamin, how kind.' Georgina spoke before Jeremy or Richard could respond. 'We would love you to coach Jeremy. We'll talk later about your fee and it would be brilliant if you could come over to our place. You can both make as much noise as you like. There are no neighbours to disturb.' She put her hand on my arm in a gesture of friendliness. Yes, I liked being touched by Georgina. Things were looking up.

*

Jeremy's playing was quite reasonable. He didn't seem to have picked up any bad habits and we made some real progress by the second session. The drawing room, as they called their lounge, certainly lent itself to recitals. Georgina walked in carrying a tray laden with a cafetière, three mugs and a plate of designer biscuits. As she poured the coffee, I pointed to the closed baby grand in front of the French windows.

'When did you last play?'

'Not played for ages,' she said. 'I really ought to, especially now that Jeremy is at university and Mark away at school. I do have the time.'

'Why don't you play with us, too, Mum? Benjamin could dig out something easy that we could all go at together.'

Georgina looked uncertain.

'Perhaps you could spend the next few days practising when you've time, so you're up to speed when I next come over?' Still she hesitated.

'Please, Georgina, it would be good fun.' I liked saying her name. Suddenly, more than anything, I wanted her to become part of our group, to share the intimacy of the music, and for me to get to know her.

*

I badly wanted to call her. I picked up the phone, then replaced it. What was I doing? This was not a good move. It had been only a week since Jeremy went back to uni for the summer term but already I was missing our sessions where the three of us created music and laughed. Not always great music but that wasn't the objective. And now I had to admit that it wasn't the playing that I missed. It was Georgina that drew me back to that house.

'Hi, it's Benjamin.'

'Hallo Benjamin.' I heard her smile.

'It's important you keep up the practice while Jeremy is away, otherwise we'll be back to square one next holiday.'

'Oh, I wonder if it's worth it. I'm not sure that I'll ever get back to playing to any decent standard. Since our sessions, I've tried to play a bit each day, but I'm not that good at motivating myself.' Was that my lead in? Was she flirting or did I just want her to?

'I could get over to see you with some duets, if you'd like?' There was a brief silence as she considered the suggestion. I willed her to agree.

'Thank you, Benjamin. I would like.'

*

'Look, the first time we play this, it's bound to go slowly,' I reassured her as she flung her arms up in frustration. I stood beside her as she leant into the keyboard, intent on her fingering. I'd come to recognise her perfume, but that day, whether because I was closer or she was nervous, the scent was even stronger. Her arms and wrists, fluid, sensual as her fingers stroked the keys. I wanted to touch her, kiss the back of her neck, take her.

The strength of the urge took me aback. This was mad, professional suicide. I tried to distract myself by looking around the room, expensively elegant, just as I imagined the rest of this house. Richard's house. I feared that if she took her eyes off the music she'd be in no doubt of what I desired at that moment. I edged backwards to stand behind her but my eagerness was becoming increasingly obvious.

'Look, I'm really sorry, but I'm not feeling brilliant,' I said, interrupting her playing. I dropped my violin and held it strategically in front of me. 'I have to get back and we're in rehearsal this afternoon, so I'm afraid ...' I knew my excuse sounded lame, but I had to escape. Screwing a sponsor's wife? Even if the union supported me, the management would want me out.

That afternoon I sat in my flat, drinking wine to help me think it through. I'd felt an intangible response from Georgina but how far could I go? Seize the day or think of my career? What would Oma have advised? I concluded that with her early history of sadness probably she would choose to follow the heart.

I lay on my bed, eyes wide open, the iPod set to repeat: the *Adagietto,* Mahler Five, my refuge.

*

Next day, the phone rang. Georgina. Was I feeling better? Resume this morning?

After the call I stood for a moment, savouring the stirred excitement, then headed for the shower. As the shampoo was rinsed from my hair, I worked out which shirts were clean, which needed ironing. My back arched under the hot jet of water.

*

Despite her practising, if she'd actually done any, the Schumann was not coming together and my mind wandered back to my feelings of the previous day.

'Oh for God's sake,' she closed the lid of the piano. 'Let's eat, I've had enough.' I followed her into the kitchen. The granite worktops, the Aga, it must have cost a fortune. I felt uneasy being there alone with her. Jeremy had told me how this was the hub of his family's daily life. I felt Richard's presence in the wealth of the place.

I leant against the wall so that I could watch her move around the softly lit room. I could never understand why people bothered to build conservatories then stuck up blinds to keep the sun out. That day the diffused light was kind to a woman of her age. She walked across a shaft of light through the open door of the conservatory and was caught momentarily in silhouette. So, she's not wearing a bra. I felt myself stir and shifted my position.

'Here, take this please and would you get the wine from the fridge?'

Our fingers touched for the first time as she handed me the corkscrew. Her hands trembled slightly. She felt it too. God, I wanted to take her up against the wall there and then but, no, not yet. Instead I took the chilled Chablis from the fridge. Carefully I screwed in the spiral. This was not the moment to end up with a broken cork. Georgina stood with her back to me, leaning against the scrubbed wooden table. Why the pause, what was she thinking?

Her silence was her signal. I removed my left hand from the ice-cold bottle and stroked my wet fingers down her bare neck. Georgina's body convulsed with a deep shiver and she gasped. I got rid of the wine bottle and moved closer in, pressing my body against hers. I reached forwards and through the fine fabric cupped her breasts in my cold hands. She shuddered and pressed back against me.

*

He readies himself for the coming storm. The conductor turns towards Benjamin's section, first urging on the racing strings, then the wind players, their instruments held high, the sound projected upwards to the audience high in the circle. Chords thunder, the insistent trumpet call dies away, echoed by the bassoon. Down and down, hopeless, the kettle-drum's muffled beat sounds. The concert hall jars with the full weight of the brass, before the lone flute and violins bring the movement to the softest of closures, like dust floating in sunlight.

Mahler's music mirrors the violinist's life: complex, punctuated by splendid highs but despairing lows. As the conductor's baton falls to rest, despite himself, Benjamin looks up, conscious of Georgie's eyes boring into him. Even at this distance he feels the ice.

Chapter Four – Jeremy's Story

Jeremy's shoulders stiffen, his fingers flex. He shares the tension of the musicians, though his stress is based in anger, not apprehension. Leaning forwards, he has a better view of the brass, ranged just a couple of meters below where he sits on the choir benches. He prefers to sit here if the chorus is not performing so he can study the conductor full on. What's more, they're the cheapest tickets in the house.

His private game is to spot the opening soloist. Jeremy identifies the trumpet player who repeatedly licks his lips, brings the instrument to his mouth, lowers it again and tosses his head with a nervous tic. In moments, this trumpeter will open the symphony with an exposed solo, the clarion call Jeremy recognises so well.

The portly conductor steps onto the podium, bows to the audience and raises his baton. So begins the piece of music which for ever will resonate with the lowest point of Jeremy's life.

Mouth dry, hands clenched, Jeremy relishes the trepidation of this moment, whether performing or listening. His skin tingles to that summoning trumpet, joined first by the broad, slow sweeps of violin bows and then by the whole orchestra in a death march that shudders forwards like a broken man following the coffin of a loved one.

*

Shit, shit, shit. Why won't the bloody steward let me into the hall? Through the closed doors I heard the applause signalling the conductor's arrival to the platform. I could have slipped into my seat as he took his bow.

'Really sorry, sir,' said the skinny girl, no older than me, as she barred my way. 'Your ticket is for the choir seats overlooking the back of the orchestra so you'd be in full view of the whole audience. I'm afraid it would be too distracting to allow you in at the last minute. I hope you understand.'

Why didn't she get it? I was perfectly happy to sit on the stairs to the side of the choir. But no, thanks to Miss Big Knickers, I'd no option other than to wait in the foyer until the interval, listening to the concert through muffling doors, watching a miniature orchestra on the black and white monitor.

It was some tosser in a Honda that made me late. Not a serious accident, but just enough to screw up the traffic on the Bristol Road. If we'd been closer in, I'd have got off the bus and run for it, but I just had to sit there as we inched around the arguing drivers. When I raced into New Street station, my train north showed 'Closed' on the departure board. *Shit, shit, shit.*

*

Jeremy leans forwards, elbows resting on knees, and looks down onto the orchestra. As the strings spell out the underlying threat, he sees Benny in profile at his desk amongst the second violins. He feels the anger choke in his throat and he transmits waves of invective towards the violinist. The music shudders again on a downward note.

The music changes into the lilt of the folk melody. The girl on Jeremy's left rocks gently to the rhythm. He frowns. Doesn't she realise that seated up here in the choir, she is a distraction for the audience facing them.

Despite his tension he is gratified to see that the hall is practically full. Not surprising for a performance of Mahler's Fifth Symphony. Visconti's *Death in Venice* to thank for that. His gaze passes over the rows of faces stretching way to the back of the ground floor, then sweeps up to the circle, the upper circle and the vertiginously raked grand tier. Reluctantly he looks over to his left to the circle ledge where his parents regularly sit. His jaw sets as he sees his mother, impassive as ever. His father slouches in his seat, face flushed and looking for all the world as though he'd just run the length of the town. Jeremy is shocked and pulls back behind the girl, out of their line of sight.

*

I am totally shot. Since the weekend, I've hardly slept. My head was still spinning this morning when I walked into the exam hall. The two hours passed like a dream as I auto-piloted through the paper. I struggled to block out what I discovered Sunday morning and to focus on the questions. I'm bound to fail.

Yesterday was shit. Impossible to revise. Head full of shrieking stuff. What to do? Nothing? Confront her? Confront them both? Whatever I decide, it's bound to be wrong. I always get things wrong.

I went on-line and spotted tonight's concert. It was pretty likely that Mum had booked tickets. With Dad in the middle of some sort of deal, I half hoped that he wouldn't be here, and maybe I could talk to her privately on the way home. Benny would be playing so I'd be able to challenge him first, before facing Mum.

Last night I lay awake, rehearsing what I'd say to each of them. To empty my head, I listened to Barenboim's Chopin nocturnes on my iPod. Eventually I drifted off.

The Ride of the Valkyries on my phone alarm woke me at half-six this morning. I felt crap but I simply had to make the call to Mum before she switched on her phone for the day. I rehearsed the words then left my voice message.

I started strongly. 'I have to see you. I'm coming home tonight. Maybe I'll see you after the concert. Otherwise, I want you to stay up for me. I need to talk after Dad has gone to bed.' Despite my efforts, my voice broke as I choked back tears. 'We've got to sort this out.'

*

The trumpets proclaim again and Jeremy winces on behalf of the woodwind players seated in front of the high decibel brass and timpani. Again the shuddering steps of the funeral march before the soft voices of the violins float words of solace. Who can offer him that now? His world is falling apart and who cares?

*

How do I climb out of this mess? Who can I talk to? Nobody at uni. Mark? No way. Mima? Would his grandmother understand? The French don't shock easily when it comes to matters of sex. Nanna, on the other hand, with her northern roots would be horrified by it all.

Mima would listen to me and be honest with her opinion. Dear old Mima, I owe her a lot, though she only really became interested in me when I was old enough for prep school. Up until then, she seemed a bit distant when we went to stay. I was fascinated by the rambling Victorian house where Poppa had his surgery. Their home was permeated by the smell of the practice, a unique blend of clinical cleanliness and decades of manila folders full of the incidentals and traumas of his patients.

'Jeremy, you must not stare at the patients when they arrive. They may be very sick and are not wishing the curious gaze of a small boy.' Mima's English was almost perfect grammatically, but I loved her French inflection and the way she spoke my name, with a soft J and open e. *Jé ré mi*. I would repeat it inside my head and feel special. It wasn't often that I felt special.

It was Mima who cajoled Gramps into paying for my violin lessons when I was a day boy at prep school. Only recently have I discovered that they'd paid my school fees too, and Mark's now, I guess. Music was always around. Dad would play his CDs really, really loud when in a bad mood, usually after we'd gone to bed. And Mima used to take me and Mark to children's concerts at the Royal Festival Hall. When I was little, the front room at our house in Parson's Green was out of bounds. Mum's baby grand took up much of the space, even though she never had time to play. Now she's got all the space in the world for it. If it weren't for that bloody piano ...

At the end of my first term I announced the good news.

'Miss Benson, my music teacher, she's been trying us with all different instruments and she thinks I'd be good at violin.' My parents exchanged looks. I was sure they would say no.

'That sounds excellent,' said Mum to my relief. 'Will you need to practise every day?' Her voice tried to remain enthusiastic. I grinned.

'Miss Benson told me to tell you straightaway that I can stay on at school for an hour to do my practice there. She doesn't want me to disturb the neighbours.'

'It was more your poor loving family that I was concerned about,' said Dad. 'So, do we look forward to you winning Young Musician of the Year in five years' time?' Mum frowned and laughed. Dad was being Dad, ambitious as ever. But, to everyone's surprise, including mine, I picked it up quite quickly and, with the help of extra tuition, I made good progress. Then came boarding school.

*

Was it during those over-lap years at boarding school when Mark first suspected I was gay? From around thirteen I felt adrift, confused by my emotions. I knew I was different. Could anyone else see that?

Then there was Grainger. I took care to keep my feelings for him well below the radar. Despite being in the same year and house as me, we had nothing else in common. He was a sporty type with little time for music or books, other than those he was forced to read. Our paths crossed during community work when we were expected to go into the local town once a week to 'do good things'. Actually it was all pretty easy stuff and I suppose we did make a difference to some people. Grainger and I were tasked to read to the wrinklies in the old people's home down by the river.

Walking to and from the home, we talked incessantly and gradually we became each other's confidante. On Sunday afternoons we would meet up and on cold wet days we would find somewhere quiet around the school where we could just hang out. It never grew into anything physical. Both of us were too shy for that. I wanted to touch him but didn't dare approach him. Maybe he thought the same. I shall never know. Between us lay something unspoken.

It came to an abrupt end during our last term. Our A levels were done and we had a couple of weeks to kick around before heading off home for good. There were trips organised to 'enrich us culturally' and some I enjoyed, like the day in London at Tate Modern. The place is awesome. On the other hand, a day hiking over some nearby moorland didn't appeal to me and, as Grainger had crocked his ankle, we stayed behind.

On the river bank there was a spot where rhododendron bushes created a wind break and privacy too, truth be told. I took my iPod with me and we just sprawled out on the grass, sharing the two ear-pieces, listening to music, something light and classical I seem to remember. Occasionally we talked and swigged on a couple of illicit beers. This had to be heaven. I rolled over on my side to face him.

'I don't suppose we'll see much of each other after next week.' The statement was an oblique question. He in turn rolled towards me. I was very aware of his closeness. It excited and frightened me. He pulled the ear-piece free and reached over to remove its pair from my ear. His fingers stroked my cheek in doing so. My heart pounded as my desire was aroused.

'No, I suppose not,' he responded with a rueful smile. 'I shall never forget you.'

He lay back and gazed up at the clouds ambling across the sky. 'I imagine you and I will always find it hard to fit in.'

He voiced the fear that rasped away in my darkest moments. What I felt wasn't normal. It certainly wasn't what I'd expected from life. Although we had never talked of being gay, tacitly we both knew it.

'Do you think we can be happy? I'm frightened of being lonely. Loads of people never come out and live life as families expect. What must that be like? Marrying, having children, while living a lie.' I imagined the expectations of my own family.

'I think I'll tell my folks after my first term at uni,' said Grainger. 'That way I won't have to go back home again if they take it badly.'

I thought about how Dad would react, remembering how he made derogatory comments about 'batting for the other side'. It was at that point that we heard approaching voices and suddenly three younger boys rounded the corner. Instinctively we rolled apart although we had hardly been touching and as I recognised Mark among the group, to my horror, I blushed.

The three stopped some yards away and just stared uneasily at us. Nobody spoke for a moment then Grainger, grinning, waved his empty beer can at them.

'No point in reporting us for drinking, guys. In a week we're out of here and in a few years' time it'll be your turn.' He turned to me. 'Come on, let's get some food. I'm famished.'

As we stood and brushed down our clothes, I felt Mark's curious eyes upon me.

'Hi,' I wound the ear-piece wiring around my i-Pod as I approached him. 'Mum phoned this morning to confirm what time she's picking us up. Did she call you too?'

He continued staring, showing no emotion.

'No, but I wouldn't expect her to. As long as she's told her first-born, duty done.'

He shrugged and walked away, the two other boys following him. As they rounded the corner of the bushes he looked back briefly. Still that blank look.

Mark never referred to that day, but I knew that he had understood. Initially I feared that he would say something at home. He never did. I'm sure I'd have realised if he'd spoken to Mum or Dad. Did I feel grateful or did I suspect that one day he might use that knowledge?

He mystified me, still does. Is he jealous that I'm the older son? I'm not aware that I'm the favourite. So why does he give Mum such a hard time? He's ace at dumb insolence.

That day with Grainger was the watershed. I'd suspected but never admitted to myself that I could be gay. By acknowledging the fact, even only indirectly, brought a calm, albeit spiked with fear of discovery.

What would university bring? Once down in Birmingham I watched and waited to see if that spark might be kindled, perhaps by a fellow student. Instead, when the moment arrived, the ensuing flames burnt us all.

*

Beside Jeremy, the girl shifts in her seat and he glances at her for the first time, seeing a slim figure and longish blond hair. He follows her gaze and is surprised to see it fixed in the direction of the circle ledge where his parents sit. His mother stands out from the crowd in a vibrant pink summer dress with a large floral pattern, her arms protected against the air-conditioning by an emerald green cardigan. To his eyes, she looks brassy. She watches the orchestra while his father faces the audience in the body of this vast hall. Jeremy speculates on what his father seeks.

*

Dad has done well. No doubt about it. From modest beginnings, bright, hard-working, ambitious. But, there has always been something about his past that niggles him. Not big enough for a chip on his shoulder, more a splinter. Now I understand how much it mattered to Dad to come back to his home territory having 'done good' in London and married the stunning, half-French daughter of a GP. Building a nationally recognised consultancy set him apart from the majority of his old school friends; except for Tony Mulligan, who had also headed south and created a thriving company. Funny how they had both ended up in the same line of business, given that there was no love lost between them. Nanna had never understood that.

'Up until they started senior school they were good friends. Then all of a sudden Tony stopped coming round and your Dad never spoke of him again.' Nanna was at her chattiest when I helped her clear away after the rare family Sunday lunch at their large Edwardian terrace house, where she and Grandad had lived for ever.

'Years later, it was Tony's mum who told me that, like your Dad, he'd worked for Bill Edwards before going down to London. Apparently, to the same place your Dad went, but your Dad never said. You could tell she was right proud of her Tony. Good thing that. She looked worn out, poor soul. Not surprising with all those kids then her husband passing over so young.'

Today Dad moves and grooves with the local mafia. That's my name for the rich set that turns up in the society pages of the local rag: well-upholstered self-satisfied men accompanied by slim-line blondes, usually trophy wife number two. I used to think it was amazing that Mum and Dad were still together but in their case Mum was already wife Number Two; wife Number One being his work. I can't imagine he's ever had time to get off with other women. And there's his 'position', as he calls it, to protect. He's known, respected, if not always liked, and right now he'll be searching among the audience to spot anyone of influence so that he can buttonhole them after the concert.

Christ Almighty, the irony of it. She's the one playing away. He hasn't a bloody clue what's going on right under his nose. Well, as she's screwed up my world, then he'll bloody well share the pain too. It's pay-back time for all those years when we all came second to 'the job'. Let's see how he reacts when he finds out she's been fucking 'his' violinist.

*

The orchestra reaches a climax which diminishes slowly, slowly. Jeremy's flare of anger subsides as the solo trumpet calls repeatedly, ever more distant, until a lone flute sounds its thin note of hope and the movement ends on a breath of strings. He, too, lets out an involuntary sigh, almost a sob, and he feels the curious eyes of the girl beside him.

Chapter Five – The Girl's Story

The girl moves her long legs sideways to allow a young man to pass. She shuffles her copious green bag under the seat as he sits down beside her, up behind the orchestra. She looks out across the hundreds of faces turned towards her, feels somewhat exposed and wishes she were wearing trousers or a longer skirt. She clamps her knees together but it is doubtful she will sustain that position for long.

The lights dim, the audience goes quiet before breaking into polite applause as the conductor walks on stage. He lifts his arms and she sees instruments raised. Just below her, a trumpet call erupts. It takes her by surprise and she is struck by its sadness.

This is going to be dire. Let's get it over with. The final part of the plan.

She shivers with anticipation. She knows what she has to do.

*

Last night, wide awake in that sterile hotel room, I played out this evening over again. What I will say to him. His likely excuse.

Over the years I've fought the bitterness. It doesn't get you anywhere. But in the last week finally I've found a focus for what's pissed me off for so long. It goes back to those early years at school when I realised I was different. Not different like Carena. Carena was black and the only Afro-Caribbean girl in 2B and in any case by the next year there were other black kids and Asians too. Not different like Shane, whose parents had split in a shitty divorce. Later there were loads of kids who quickly learnt the advantages of two families.

I had no Dad. Never had. From the beginning there was just me and Mum. It was only when other kids started to get at me that I even began to think about it.

'Why don't I have a Dad?' I asked as Mum drove away from my primary school through the wet darkness. I was one of the handful of kids who stayed behind after school when no parent or responsible adult could get back from work to collect us any earlier. I quite liked sitting reading books and comics, occasionally listening to music. Mum always arrived last, smartly dressed but looking fraught.

'You just don't.' Out of the corner of my eye I saw Mum glance at me as she changed gear and swung into the main road. 'Shall we stop and pick up a pizza?' An old trick to distract me.

'Great.' I wasn't going to turn down that offer, but equally she wasn't going to put me off. 'Though when we get home I'm going to ask you again.'

*

Christ, this all sounds so dreary.

The chap beside her leans forwards and rests his elbows on his knees. He stares down into the orchestra. She can only see the backs of most of the players, but some of the violinists are half turned towards her. Their eyes are fixed on the music stands before them. She watches the conductor waving his arms, a pointer in his right hand.

The music switches tempo and the girl starts to sway to the gentle lilt.

This is more like it.

She stops moving as she senses a glare from the guy on her right, who sits rigid in his seat.

OK, got the message. Fucking prick. Twenty something going on fifty.

*

Classical music has never been my thing. There was music around the house from when I was a kid and I remember Mum picking me up and dancing around the lounge to Lionel Ritchie until I was nearly sick and shrieked to get down or I'd wet myself. Then there were the CDs she played when a fella came to collect her. I would hover at the top of the stairs hoping to get a sight of him. Was this one going to drop by again? Would he take me down to see the big ships come into port? Would he be my Dad one day? None of them ever did. None of them ever was.

Except The Bear. He was always there from my earliest memory. Not every week, sometimes not for weeks at a time. Whenever he came, he always brought me something. Coloured crayons, a reading book, nothing grand. And Mum always got flowers, which she always seemed to dismiss as a bit of nonsense, though later she always changed the water in the vase and picked off the dead flower heads.

He was The Bear because he was round and cuddly, like the teddy bear he gave me when I was a kid.

At one time, I used to pretend he was my Dad. Until that day when Mum finally gave in to the questions. I was eleven and I suppose she felt I was old enough to be told the truth. Well some of it. It was the summer holidays before I went up to my next school, the local comp, which had a mixed reputation both for the kids who went there and academically.

'Most of your friends will be going there too,' she said. 'So this time there's no need to get uptight about bullying.'

'But it'll be worse this time. Everyone's used to divorced parents now, even a Dad that's buggered off, but if I don't even know who my Dad was, they'll call you a slag for getting up the duff. If you don't tell me, then I'll say The Bear is my Dad.'

'You must never talk about him, not to anybody. Do you hear? And stop that language. I don't like it.' Mum getting snappy was rare. And I hated it. It frightened me. Why hadn't she put me up for adoption from day one? It was too late for that by then, wasn't it? She held down a reasonable job, but I suppose having me around her neck did hold her back. If she hadn't needed to get home to me after school, she probably could have done even better. But she wouldn't ever have put me into care. The Bear wouldn't have let her.

'Your Dad was a clever, good-looking man and he fell in love with me but couldn't marry me because he'd promised to marry someone else. But he didn't love her as much as me. And when I discovered I was expecting you, he explained he couldn't have two families. It wouldn't be fair to either. So we agreed that he would send me money and I could look after you on my own.'

'Didn't he ever want to see me?'

'He said it was best that you never met so you wouldn't get upset.'

At eleven that was a lot to take in.

Only in recent years, after relationships of my own, have I realised how she sugared the pill that day. What a load of crap. But then I wanted to believe it.

Telling fibs, telling lies, deceit. It's all part of what we do. *Better not to know. Don't want you to be hurt.* We kid ourselves it's for the best, unless we're on the receiving end.

*

I wonder where he's sitting? I followed him all the way here but lost him when I picked up our tickets. Probably in the expensive seats though I don't see him near the front.

*

The wanker gave us just enough to scrape through. Bet his kids didn't go without.

I suppose today they'd call it a 'staycation'. I call it not being able to afford to go away on holiday. Mum would take time off work and we'd go out and do something every day, usually along the south coast but sometimes in London. I liked going up on the train and walking through Waterloo station right onto the South Bank. Mum knew her way around. She worked there before I was born. It's where she met 'him'.

Although short, the best holidays were when The Bear used to take us away for a couple of nights. Center Parc was my favourite and I could play with other kids while Mum and The Bear went off and did other stuff. I suppose that's when they had sex. Though to this day I've never seen him stay overnight with Mum.

*

Wow, those trumpets and things are loud. What must it be like for the players sitting in front of them? 'Elf and Safety' would have something to say.

There's that bit again from the beginning. Sounds like someone's funeral. How fucking appropriate. Can't wait to get this plan rolling out.

*

The bullying never happened at the new school. I determined from the first day that I'd never be bullied again. True, most of my classmates already knew me and the lack of a father was no longer an issue. But Amanda was a newcomer to the area and coped with her puppy fat problem by picking on the shortcomings of others. I was ready for her.

It was during break on a rainy winter's day that Amanda got the point. Friends told me she'd asked about my family and discovered the story of my 'unknown' father. Banned from the wet playground, we all hung about in damp groups, crushed against the radiators in the staircase atrium. We talked about those we despised; who was the coolest boy band of the day; who fancied who; was Matthew gay? As a new arrival, Amanda didn't really belong to any set and that day latched onto ours.

'Why don't you know who your Dad is?' It came from nowhere. I tried the withering, 'I can't be arsed to reply' look, but she persisted. 'Did your mother have so many men she wasn't sure who it was? There's DNA testing now so you could find out.'

When Mum arrived, she was furious. She'd been in an important meeting. She was always in important meetings. She'd had to explain to her boss that there was a problem at her daughter's school. I suppose in those days it underlined the disadvantages of employing a single mother. She just didn't need this.

Amanda will always have problems with her little finger. Typing must be a bit difficult and she'll never play a music instrument. No idea where the thought came from to grab that chubby hand and bend the little finger back until I heard the crack. God, I hated her and all the bullies before her.

Nobody asked about my Dad again.

*

The music builds again into a storm and she is fascinated by the violinists.

Why do they need so many? My God, they work hard at this. She sees the string players' elbows flash back and forth, the bows flying high, their bodies rocking with the effort. It sounds desperately sad.

That trumpet again, though not so loud this time, and the brass wades in and blasts away. Her eyes wander again around the auditorium, this time studying the faces peering over the balcony of the side ledges. Her gaze drops down to the ledge running level with her own seat and she stiffens.

There he is. Which is his wife? Not the grey haired woman to his right. It must be the one on his other side. The girl's jaw sets. *Good looking, expensively dressed. Fuck you, fuck you both. Just wait, poor cow.*

The music softens through a distant trumpet call, a flute pleading forlornly, then the strings bring the movement to a gentle close. The girl rages inwardly and hardly hears the movement subside. In the silence that follows, she hears a half sob from the guy besides her and she looks at his profile; a desperate look sets his face.

SECOND MOVEMENT

Stürmisch bewegt

Chapter Six – Richard's Story

Mahler's black mood continues as the orchestra surges into the stormy second movement. Georgina's evident distress takes Richard by surprise.

He frowns with irritation. *What the hell's wrong? Mahler always gets to her but the really weepy bit isn't until the fourth movement.*

He shifts his gaze back to the platform and shrinks further into his chair. *She can't have discovered the deal is going pear-shaped. So, what else, for God's sake?* He reassures himself that Georgina knows instinctively when not to interfere and leave him to concentrate on the business.

*

At an early stage in our marriage I made it quite clear to Georgina that there were times when I needed to be left alone. Selfish? Very possibly but also necessary. If I was going to succeed, I couldn't afford to take my eye off the ball.

Like the time Conningsbury pitched for the Fairhampton project. I'd worked my balls off cultivating contacts even to get to pitch. Because of the many listed buildings, it was a complicated traffic plan and involved liaison with the town's heritage groups. I really enjoyed getting stuck into all that and I discovered some useful people on the conservation side. The leader of the group, Pat Thomas helped build bridges with the people who can so often scupper a development project. Sure, they didn't like everything we proposed but, if Conningsbury were to win the scheme, I had to demonstrate to the planners that we'd covered all bases. If I could get even warm support from the locals, we stood a chance of gaining the contract.

I spent many evenings and even some weekends with Pat and her colleagues walking the streets, discussing their concerns. It meant Georgina was stuck at home in Palmers Green with two very young boys but, since she didn't make a fuss, other than expressing some frustration, I suppose I rather took advantage. Instead of driving straight back into London after a meeting, I'd catch a bowl of pasta with Pat, initially in a local Italian, then in her chaotic terraced house on the edge of the old town. Pat was at least ten years older than me but had great charisma. She would have been part of the hippy generation. Striking, rather than beautiful, she'd been married and divorced twice.

One Saturday afternoon, after a morning meeting with the conservationists, we ended up in bed. Georgina had opted to take the kids to her parents in Berkshire for the weekend and I was due to drive over to their place straight from Fairhampton. When I turned up early evening, excusing my lateness somewhat lamely, I felt the questioning eyes of her mother. A French woman must have a sixth sense for infidelity.

Did I feel guilty cheating on Georgina? Not really. Well, it meant nothing, just a one-off. I loved Georgina, for God's sake. Pat probably had lots of lovers and I was just one of many. I must confess though that it was more with thoughts of the increasing spread of AIDS rather than a question of fidelity that I avoided a repeat performance. What Georgina didn't know wouldn't hurt her, would it?

*

Georgina is that strange mixture of soft emotion blended with a toughness that surprises many. Music can touch her but she gets most worked up about the kids. Once, when Jeremy was still at boarding school, out of the blue she questioned whether it was in his best interests to continue there. Our discussion became quite heated.

'Of course he should bloody well stay on. It's the best education he could possibly hope for and thanks to your parents we have it on a plate. Do you really want him to go the local comp? He's not the sharpest knife in the box and I've serious doubts that he'll make much of himself academically.'

She turned to me, her eyes flashing. 'Don't you ever, ever dare put him down like that. Just because he's sensitive and you're not!' She glared at me as her eyes welled. I waited for her to blink and the tears to flow but remarkably she held my gaze before gathering up a load of freshly dried towels and sweeping out of the kitchen, not a tear spilt.

Sensitivity? That stung, but sensitivity don't butter no parsnips, as Mum would say.

*

Has Georgina somehow discovered what mess the company is in? Tom's wife, Christine, attends the same music appreciation group as Georgina. Has he gossiped about the deal at home and is Christine gagging to show-off her insider knowledge to the boss's wife? Like the fact that twice this year I've not drawn a salary so we could pay the wages bill. Has she made some arsy comment to Georgina? Bitch.

And how the fuck did Mulligan know that now would be a good time to make a move, to make the call?

*

'Rich!' Mulligan's crisp address took me aback. My PA was away from her desk and one of the team had fielded the incoming call and batted it straight to my phone without checking if I'd take it. I swore inwardly and responded without warmth. He requested a meeting to discuss something of mutual benefit. I doubted it but agreed to call him when next in London.

'No need, Rich,' he persisted. 'I'm seeing Mum next weekend so I'll come up Friday morning and take you for lunch.' I reflected but quickly recognised that this meeting was going to happen, so better sooner than later.

We met at a restaurant of his choosing, expensive but not flash. If Mulligan was seeking to demonstrate his acquisition of taste over the years, he succeeded at least in this. He was already in the bar as I arrived punctually, his glass charged with a gin and tonic. I hadn't seen him for some years and he'd thickened out, which, being on the short side, didn't suit him. He didn't stand as I approached and from above I could see that his hair had thinned appreciably. He waved me to the seat opposite him. Imperious git.

Initially the talk was general, about his mother, long time a widow. Although he'd lived in the South for more years than I, he hadn't lost any of his northern accent. I knew that I still retained a slight twang, more pronounced when agitated, despite the efforts of my mother to 'better myself', and, I confess, an early wish to distance myself from the industrial North.

He talked broadly about the effect of the economy on the civil engineering sector and commented disparagingly on some high profile projects which had been shelved.

'We were crapping ourselves that we wouldn't get the go-ahead on the East London project but the knock-on from the Olympics meant that there was no going back at this stage, so they signed us up, good as gold.' I nodded my acknowledgement of their good fortune. A week earlier I'd read about their win in the trade press. Lucky bastards.

As I was finishing an exceedingly good steak and remembering how he had always gobbled his food as a kid, probably essential in a large household, he pushed away his cleared plate, sat back and lobbed his grenade.

'I've come up to make you an offer for your business, Richard.' The use of my full name underlined the genuineness of his proposition. 'Things are going like a train down south but the only way to make a step-change is through acquisition, or merger.' His smile was condescending.

'What makes you think we're for sale?' I placed the knife and fork together on my plate and pushed away the unfinished meal in a gesture of dismissal.

'The word is out that you're in trouble,' he smiled ruefully. 'It would be a tragedy to see Bill's business go under after he entrusted it to you, Rich.'

'That's bullshit. We're not in trouble. Nobody is trading brilliantly in this climate.' As I spoke, I remembered his practice was bucking the trend.

I removed my glasses and concentrated on polishing them. Mulligan continued to press his case while my mind raced. I was furious to be put into this position, recognising that a merger would probably be the only way out of the shit. But not with Mulligan. I couldn't trust him. Not after what happened with Melanie.

*

Not sure when Melanie first came onto the scene but she soon latched onto Conningsbury's drinking sessions after work. She was attractive in what Georgina would call a *jolie-laide* sort of way. But pushy with it. Mulligan hit on her straight-away and the two of them would peel off around six thirty, heading, I presumed, to his flat. It was when Mulligan was away working on a project down in the West Country that I got to know her. Really got to know her. When Mulligan returned, Melanie made it clear to him that she'd moved on. I couldn't help myself. I was jubilant. I'd got one over him, the tosser. His reaction was predictable and working relations became ever more strained.

*

The wistful folk song closes and develops into a country festival which whirls out of control. In a cascade of sound, the whole orchestra again plunges headlong into the depths. With wide-swept bowing, the strings draw the listeners into calmer side waters.

Richard feels a vibration against his right hip. An incoming message to his phone. He itches to check who sent it, but dares not incur Georgina's wrath. The woman sitting to his right is turned away from him, intent on the orchestra. It might be Mulligan; few people text him at this time of the evening. Unless it's one of the boys with a problem, though they usually call their mother.

*

Mulligan probably bore a grudge from that day when he overheard Dad's disparaging view of him and his family, but he never forgave me for taking Melanie. He was so cocky, he never dreamt she wouldn't be there waiting for him when he returned from setting up the Taunton job. I'd always quite fancied her, and with Mulligan away, somehow she became even more desirable. Not that I'd set out to put one over on him, but that first night I got her into bed there was an element of triumph mixed with the sex. There was something of the animal about Melanie which drew me back a second and third time. To her, sex was natural, to be enjoyed to the full. And we had a good time together. Bars, clubs, dancing, she was up for it.

As the time drew nearer to Mulligan's return I taunted her with a grin.

'Well, you'd best enjoy this last week. It's make your mind up time. Him or me – I don't share.' I was buggered if I'd share with Mulligan.

She went quiet. 'Listen. What I do with my life is my decision. If I choose to see both of you, I shall.' I shrugged. She was more than just a good shag and the last few weeks had been bloody good but neither I nor Mulligan would share anything, let alone a woman.

Melanie didn't go into details but the showdown had been unpleasant. As our relationship continued, Mulligan stopped coming for office drinks after work when Melanie and I would hang out before heading to her flat.

It was before the Winchester pitch that I was aware Mulligan was making life difficult for me. Although I couldn't prove it, I'm convinced it was he who corrupted the file with detailed calculations needed for a client meeting I was due to front two days later. I worked through both nights to get the information together again. A close call. There were other 'mishaps' along the way which couldn't be explained but which I suspect were initiated by Mulligan.

My greatest fear of the man came after I started dating Georgina. She was good looking, not quite beautiful, and had a depth which attracted me from our first meeting. Totally different from Melanie. Class. Looking for commitment, which Melanie certainly didn't want. So, as my relationship with Georgina grew, Melanie stepped back into the shadows. Georgina would be an asset as my career advanced and there was no doubt in my mind that it would.

Melanie had been restless for some time and increasingly her work was taking her out of London. Georgina and I went to a few concerts, always followed by a meal. Initially, nothing more. Such a contrast to party girl Melanie. Maybe I was growing up, but I liked this new option and when I eventually got Georgina to bed, the sex was generous, warm.

I was up front with Melanie and she appeared unconcerned. 'Fine. She's more your future than I am, anyway. A pity though to miss out on what we do have,' she grinned. I half wondered if she would take up again with Mulligan. Although I had relinquished my 'rights', it would have pissed me off big time if she had.

My relationship with Georgina grew. I met her parents: he jovially appraising, she icily assessing. I'm still not sure whether Colette has ever approved of me.

Melanie stepped out of the limelight but didn't disappear altogether. There was something irresistible about her. Sex with Melanie was something else, addictive, and although Georgina and I were soon sleeping together, Melanie wasn't totally out of my life. I had an uneasy fear that colleagues, especially Mulligan, might be aware of this liaison. I wouldn't have wanted Georgina to find out.

Over the next year I managed to see Melanie if not for a whole night, at least for the occasional evening, with an unpredictable and unwished for outcome.

A month before my wedding, she and I met at the usual bar in Pimlico. She looked unusually stressed for someone normally laid back and got straight to the point.

'You're not going to like this. I'm pregnant.'

I felt sick and couldn't think what to say. For Christ's sake, she was on the pill, wasn't she? She continued in a flat voice, saying how she'd just been accepted for a job in Southampton. It would be cheaper to bring up a kid outside of London. I contemplated asking if she'd considered an abortion but judged it was not the question to raise.

'So we'll have to come to some arrangement for you to look after it,' she ended. 'No, not literally,' she answered my unspoken thought. 'You marry your posh Georgina next month. I'll have the kid in around seven months' time, then you start paying me maintenance.' She paused for me to take this in. 'And I'll say nothing.'

This was the closest she got to blackmail but her meaning was clear. The regular payments started the month her daughter was born. All was neatly managed through lawyers and we never spoke again. It was the deal.

How Mulligan found out back at the beginning, I've no idea. But he did and dropped hints that he knew. When I had my stag night a week before the wedding, one of the guys from work drew me to one side.

'Just watch your back, Richard. I'd hate to see Mulligan stitch you up over Melanie.' I sobered up. What had Mulligan found out? That I was seeing her? That she was pregnant? Fuck. Double fuck.

'You've been seen having drinks with her in a bar in Pimlico, you lucky bastard,' he chortled and peeled away to get another drink. Was that it? Was this all that people, Mulligan, knew? Keep your nerve. Just keep your nerve.

I kept my nerve and over the years nothing got out. Certainly not to Georgina. So far.

*

The storming music rages and Richard can wait no longer. The auditorium resounds with a theme reminiscent of imperial Russia. He reaches across to take the programme from Georgina's lap and opens it onto his own. His hand slips into his jacket pocket and, despite his wife's unspoken outrage, he pulls out his phone and holds it beneath the programme, hiding its illuminated screen from the darkened auditorium. He spots Mulligan's name. He needs to open the message and does so, shielding the screen from Georgina and the woman on his right.

The strings race and the woodwind point their instruments up high. The clamour subsides and brass instruments take turns to call out in gentle reproach. The wayward bows of cellos and double basses joust with each other and a single soft drum beat brings the movement to a close. Richard sits rigid and unbelieving.

Chapter Seven – Georgina's Story

The hall falls silent. The conductor crouches over the score. He raises his arms for a second then impels the orchestra into a whirling shriek, music of terror. Georgina stares into space as her tears evaporate. She waits to blink until sure that Richard's gaze has returned to the orchestra. The music subsides and soothes her with its meandering. Woodwind instruments interrupt the peace with insistent bursts, like a toddler tugging for attention at his mother's skirt. Then, like snapped patience, the strings strike in a sharp swirl of admonishment.

*

I thought back to those early days with the children. Unlike now, Mark was such a good child compared with Jeremy, who had always been needy. I turned to my mother for help though she wasn't as supportive as I expected.

'But Maman, Jeremy is three now and whinges on when I'm feeding Mark. I don't want him to feel unloved, but it's exhausting trying to cope with his constant demands for attention.'

'You make too much out of it,' said my mother with Gallic bluntness. 'Do not try to analyse your child's emotions ... or your own. Children are little animals that will take what they can and just need to be trained. Kindly, though.' Maman had no truck with the books on childcare that were swapped around mother and baby support groups.

'Don't ask me,' disclaimed Richard one evening, when I sought his view. 'Children are your department and I haven't a clue.' To my irritation he returned to his files spread over the dining table, and I sat with my eyes closed, too tired to concentrate on the motherhood magazine on my lap. Instead I focused on the calming Chopin playing in the background.

'He'll grow out of it. You see, once Mark's a toddler they'll be able to play together. And then I can get more involved, take them to the park.' I raised my eyes under my closed lids.

Nonetheless, over the years I wondered whether I'd been as patient with Jeremy as I ought? Now I question: is it my fault that he's gay?

*

Those early years with the children were not easy. I found motherhood more stifling than expected. It wasn't that I'd been a high flyer, but I had enjoyed my career, especially my job with the bank in Geneva. I couldn't afford to live in the city so commuted daily from a nearby village. Some commute. I'd walk from my tiny apartment down to the local station and breathe in that air only possible where a lake lies among mountains. The stopping train would carry me into the centre of that cosmopolitan, almost un-Swiss, city. Unfair to say un-Swiss. It was so ordered and clean, it couldn't belong to any other nation. It was just that the trains, the buses, the streets were alive with so many different tongues. I used to play the game of spot the nationality. I couldn't do it now though; so many Eastern European languages around.

I love mountains and after my A Levels I'd been torn between university in Grenoble, amidst the Savoy Alps, or Lyon. The latter proved a good choice. I enjoyed its cultural scene - and food - and I made good friends lasting to the present day. Once, before the children were born, I took Richard back there. Not a good idea. He didn't speak much French and although my friends spoke some English, the holiday was a strain and we never went back. Somewhere to return to one day, perhaps on my own. An adventure, just for me.

After a couple of years working in Geneva, I felt the need to return to the UK. I loved the life but it was a city of transition with people posted there and moved on a year or so later. None of the boyfriends turned into anything special, so when the bank offered me a transfer to their London operation, I was happy to accept. London was much bigger and dirtier in comparison but after a while I became less conscious of the pollution, the congestion, the crowding on tubes and buses.

With my experience and languages, I worked as PA to the bank's CEO, a Frenchman in his forties. He blended a ruthless business style with stereotypical French charm. Marcel was in great demand and I enjoyed my role as gatekeeper, organising his life, both professional and private. No different from most PAs, I suppose. His wife reminded me of a younger version of my mother: neat, attractive, calculating. I felt her distrust from our first meeting. Had Marcel given her past cause to suspect me? I certainly had no intention of being seduced by him.

Really, I hadn't. We travelled together quite often, usually to Geneva or Paris, sometimes to Frankfurt, even New York. Always he was charming but business-like. I never felt uncomfortable in my role. Until that last time in New York. I suppose it was the jet-lag and for both of us our guard was down. We'd arrived mid-afternoon their time and knew that it was important to stay up as long as possible the first evening to get into the rhythm and be fresh for the next day's business. Which is how we ended up in the hotel restaurant eating a meal together, something which occurred rarely.

I liked him, respected him, but had never experienced deeper feelings. I suspect that those sentiments were reciprocated. As the conversation shifted away from the job, it drifted back to earlier years, to our hopes and ambitions. He revealed his love of jazz.

'When I was at university I played sax in a band. I lived for music but my parents quickly hauled me back to reality. So here I am in the world of finance.'

I sensed regret for a lost world. That evening, as we parted in the lift, he bent towards me and kissed both cheeks, the first time his Gallic courtesy had been extended in my direction.

It was two evenings later, after his dinner companion cried off, that he suggested going to a jazz club. Not really my scene but it was vibrant and stirred all manner of emotions. The intense smoky atmosphere lifted us into a different world, perhaps a world that provoked memories of younger, more uninhibited days. In the taxi back to our hotel, Marcel took my hand and raised it to his lips. I was in no doubt of what he wanted next and in response something burned deep within me.

The next morning, as I lay half awake, his body beside me stirred. I wanted more of his gentle but confident love-making. Instead, he rose without a word and quickly dressed.

'My breakfast meeting is at eight thirty. I shall see you in the lobby at eight fifteen?' I nodded and understood. Last night was last night. Today is today and the open door was again closed.

I didn't feel shame at what had happened between us. We flew back separately, I to London, he to Geneva, and in the following weeks I questioned whether anything at all had happened. But he had awoken feelings in me, feelings that were not returned. I hadn't inherited the indifference to marital peccadillo that is supposed to be part of a Frenchwoman's psyche, be she the wife or the mistress. Not for me the *cinq à sept* after-work affair. I had to find another job.

*

The music of marching men drags her back to the now. Soon the full blast of the orchestra, clashing cymbals signalling mayhem, focuses her on what is to follow with Jeremy. There is no way out. Down and down and down, the symphony engulfs her and she wishes herself far from this place and music which accuses betrayal, infidelity.

*

Trust. Such a small word. Such a big expectation. Perhaps nobody is fully trustworthy. Everyone lies. Even within my narrow world I know that with certainty. Why should I be surprised if someone betrays me? I have betrayed others along the way. Maybe that is what life is about, weaving your way through deceit and disappointment, bouncing back time after time?

From the start, I knew that what I had with Benjamin was wrong. The enforced isolation of that summer provided unavoidable hours to debate in my head where to go with our mad affair. This really wasn't me. Nearly fifty and feeling so exhilarated one moment and squalidly ashamed the next. Middle-aged and gloriously in love again. At the same time guilty as hell for betraying my husband, my family.

With the boys back for the summer vacation there would be no opportunity for Benjamin and me to be alone, to make love. I refused to go to his home. So many other players lived in that part of the city. Discovery by one of the orchestra would be unbearably shameful. In the event, with his grandmother so ill, he joined his father in Vienna, and remained until her death.

Our last meeting, before the boys broke up, didn't go well. Perhaps already I was losing my nerve. That day his probing, which led me to reveal more of my past than I intended, raised a barrier between us that had never existed. Now it did.

I was difficult to live with, unable to settle. I snapped at everyone. My mother raised her eyebrows but did not comment when, during a visit, I thanked her and Papa, but turned down the offer of their Normandy house for a couple of weeks. I couldn't bear the thought of the four of us cooped up in that cottage yet again, with our books and our music. Our only escape would be down to the markets in nearby villages in search of local delicacies: a stinky runny Livarot cheese, Teurgoule, a heart-stoppingly delicious rice pudding, and the potent Calvados, an essential *digestif*. It was a family ritual I'd once loved. Now I felt trapped. It was mean of me but the boys, now older and with wider interests, seemed indifferent, and already Richard was withdrawing, wrapped up in his business, just as grumpy as me.

Mark's response to the news was chilling, implying we were past the years of playing 'Happy Families' in France. More disturbing to me was his suggestion that Richard and I should take holidays apart. What sparked that thought? Guilt framed my question: what does he know?

As it turned out, thank heavens we weren't tucked away in deepest Normandy, miles from the nearest hospital. My father has a high regard for the French medical system, but the location of their cottage could have been a death sentence for Richard.

Mark and Jeremy had been home only a couple of weeks and were knocking around the place, both half-heartedly trying to get holiday jobs. The weather was heavy with warm cloudy days which encouraged irritable lethargy. I was heading off to the local music appreciation group for the last meeting before the summer break. English composers was the theme and I was looking forward to snippets of Elgar, Vaughan Williams and Butterworth, ideal for summer.

My mobile rang as I drove into the village proper. I could have walked in but planned to continue on afterwards to the supermarket on the edge of town. Raw prawns in their shells, plus fresh fennel, would make a favourite risotto for tonight's supper. Without hands-free in my Audi, I let the phone ring out to voice-mail. As I drew up at the village hall I waved to a friend and pointed to my mobile as I called up my messages. The voice of Richard's secretary turned me to ice.

'Georgina, you've got to get to the Royal, as quick as you can. Richard's had a heart attack, we think. The paramedics are just putting him into the ambulance. No point coming here. I'll call you at home in case you don't have your mobile with you. Please call me back when you hear this.'

Where the calmness came from, I don't know but I re-started the engine with one hand and speed-dialled Richard's office with the other. By the time someone picked up, I was already heading off.

'It's Georgina. What's happened? Is Richard alright?' I steered through the winding lanes with my right hand and regretted no hands-free. *Please don't let him die.*

'He had pains in his chest so we called an ambulance,' said one of Richard's team. 'He's been talking to the paramedics so I'm sure he'll be alright. Just get yourself safely to the hospital and you'll see him there.'

The doctors worked on him immediately and by the end of that day they had performed a coronary angioplasty and fitted a stent. The boys joined me at Richard's hospital bedside. We were shocked to see him looking so desperately tired. Walking left him exhausted. It would take time for him to regain strength, but it was time that we had won, thanks to the medics.

The consultant that eventually discharged Richard admitted that the speedy treatment given by the ambulance team had made all the difference to the outcome.

'You were lucky. Getting to hospital quickly allowed us to sort you out. You've been given a second chance. At the same time, you need to review your diet, your exercise, your lifestyle in general.' Richard nodded his acceptance. That day he would have agreed to anything.

*

Georgina glances at Richard's profile with his receding thick hair and rimless bifocals perched half-way down his nose. She resists the urge to lean forwards and push them into place, as she would do at home in a teasing way, aware that it irritated him. His face is less florid now. She is relieved.

*

By September, Richard was making progress and went back to work, initially only three days a week. Life went on. Jeremy, hearing that Benjamin was back from Austria, asked why we didn't resume our coaching sessions for the few weeks before the end of the vacation. Remembering the content of my final voicemail message to Benjamin in Vienna, I made feeble excuses. Jeremy grumbled but let it go.

I was relieved when Mark returned to his last year at school and Jeremy headed south for his final year at uni. Mark had been particularly bolshie during the holiday and not even Richard's illness seemed to have improved his challenging behaviour. He had ended up working with Richard's book-keeper and moaned that he spent all day logging incoming invoices. I told him to be glad not to be out in all weathers working on the local farms.

On his return from Austria, Benjamin had sent a card to Richard, wishing him a speedy recovery. Beyond that there was no contact between us. Why should there be? After all, my call had ended the affair. Did I want him to ring? If he did, how would I respond? Would I weaken?

When the concert season started in the autumn, I ensured that Richard and I saw Benjamin only at public events, never just the three of us, and I avoided all eye contact. Then, just as I thought I could control my feelings, I was taken totally off-guard.

During one of my regular phone calls to Jeremy, we exchanged the usual pleasantries, then with his Tigger-like enthusiasm he pulled the rug from under me.

'Benjamin's been on the phone. He's taken up my suggestion to come down to Birmingham to hear Rattle conduct. He's mates with some of the band down here and he'd like to meet them afterwards.' I felt a sharp stab of jealousy, quite ridiculous. After all, Benjamin often said he needs to listen to other orchestras. I asked casually where he would stay and when Jeremy was evasive, I assumed it would be probably with his family.

At the time I never imagined ... Why would I? Only now do I recall how Jeremy shone with enthusiasm whenever Benjamin called round to the house for a coaching session. The words of the music master return. It was not just the music that had revved up Jeremy but at that point I didn't know what I do now.

*

Georgina responds to the imperial theme triumphing throughout the auditorium and instinctively she arches her back. The music reminds her of the transcending exhilaration of loving Benjamin, glorious sensations, intensified by their inevitable reconciliation. Her covert memories are interrupted as Richard's hand swings over and scoops up the programme from her lap. In seconds she realises what he is up to and glares at him as he fishes his phone out of his jacket pocket and slips it beneath the opened programme. He can hide the phone but not the glow from the illuminated screen as he opens a message. How could he be so crass?

Anger surges within her. Anger against Richard for behaving like a prat; anger with Benjamin for betraying her – with her son, with anyone, for God's sake. And anger against herself. How could she have got to this point?

She leans deeper into her seat as soft pastoral tones wash over her. Again the single thread of melody is echoed by violins, oboes and the mournful notes of the muted brass. Richard has switched off his phone and is looking out over the concert hall, an unhealthy pallor suffusing his face. *What the hell's wrong?* For a moment she wonders if he is unwell but her growing suspicion takes over. *What have you just read?*

The movement closes with two desolate notes, plucked from cellos and basses, and with one decisive beat of the kettle-drum.

She closes her eyes to block out the guilt.

Chapter Eight – Benjamin's Story

The conductor raises his baton and with one stroke the final calm of the first movement is shattered by the raging storm of the second. Benjamin accompanies his fellow string players into the turmoil, flashing bows semaphoring perfect terror. Woodwind shrieks as trumpets, horns and trombones compete for dominance. Benjamin hears the sound of flight, but there is no flight from the fear that has nagged him since he read Jeremy's message back-stage.

*

Contact from Jeremy was usually by text from his flash iPhone to my pay-as-you-go.

'You've got to dump that load of crap,' he would say whenever I fished out my bog-standard mobile, devoid of the fancy apps of his own phone, of course a Christmas present from Richard and Georgie.

'Fuck off,' I grinned and shrugged the first few times. More recently his sniping has pissed me off. He's like a kid who goads just to see how far he can push it.

Christ, I'd never intended to get involved with Jeremy let alone for him to 'fall in love' with me. It didn't even strike me that he could be gay until that second Birmingham concert. If I'd realised, not for one second would I have stayed over at his place. Even then, I should have had more sense and not given in to ... whatever.

So where did my life get so fucked up?

Music college was a breeze – other than being permanently skint. What an amazing crowd. Those brass players – crazy, the lot of them. And they knew how to party. Some were mates, good mates, still are. Then we had the groupies, especially the posh totty, ostensibly interested in the music, but really up for it. Great times.

Probably life changed course that night at the Barbican, the Mahler Nine. I'd been given a complimentary ticket. The piece blows me away, always does, no matter who plays or conducts. Henry was playing among the band that night and I texted him.

Meet up drink after concert?

We got to know each other when he came to college to coach some of the viola players. Mid thirties, easy-going, make you smile sort of guy.

Instead of dropping into a pub, he suggested his nearby flat. Like me, he can stay high for hours after a gig so en-route we stopped to buy wine to see us through.

'Look,' I said as we rummaged through the special offers. 'Maybe this isn't such a good idea. You must be knackered after playing for an hour and a half non-stop.' He looked at me with that gentle smile.

'God, no. I need someone to help me come down after that. Don't tell me your emotions aren't all over the place too.'

He was right. I felt stirred to the depths by the sadness of the Mahler.

'Yes, totally.' I paused as a memory surfaced. 'Last time I heard Mahler Nine was in Rome. It was magnificent. There must have been three thousand in the audience and every one totally knocked out by the piece. By the end, one of the cellists on the front row was in tears. He was Italian, though.'

He grinned back at me.

In Henry's modest flat I accepted the large glass of wine. He sat beside me on the capacious saggy sofa, covered with rugs of questionable provenance. We talked, drank, talked some more. It was just part of the unwinding we all need after a gig. Neither of us could let go the music we'd just heard and Henry enjoyed expounding his views on Mahler.

'He died so young. Fifty-one is no age. And what a life of frustration. His conducting job allowed such little time for him to compose. I'm amazed he wrote as much as he did.'

'Sure, but during the summer, didn't he take himself off to a hut by a lake, somewhere quiet to write music? Let's face it, you need your head totally clear to create, whether it's music, painting or writing.'

'Absolutely, but don't forget that on top of everything else, Mahler had to cope with the politics of Germany and Vienna at that time. Benjamin, you, with your family history, are only too well aware of the Anti-Semitism. Maybe at that time in Vienna to get the top conducting job, he had no alternative but to convert to Catholicism. A big ask, all the same. Probably hardest of all, the poor sod knew his wife was playing away. All that must have made Mahler one pretty screwed up guy.'

'Sure, yet, despite all that, he managed to write ten symphonies; well the last one was nearly finished. And his Fifth, that has to be my favourite.' I sipped my wine. 'Whenever I'm at rock bottom, I play that *Adagietto* over and over. I set my iPod to repeat, close my eyes and let it take me over. Trouble is, these days you hear it churned out as wallpaper sound-track in documentaries. Can't stand it.' My irritation threatened to disrupt the tranquillity of the moment. Henry shrugged, leant towards me and topped up my wine as I continued.

'It's all down to Visconti hijacking it for *Death in Venice*. That scene when Aschenbach dies alone on the beach. Death is a finality but for me Mahler's *Adagietto* doesn't offer that release.' Suddenly I choked out an angry sob and hot tears of embarrassment streamed from my eyes. I couldn't help myself. Where did all that come from?

Henry took the glass from my hand. He smiled and gently pulled me towards him so that my head rested on his chest, his arm loosely around me. He stroked my hair. Neither of us spoke. Maybe it was the wine, maybe it was the moment, but I didn't resist this man invading my space with such a gesture of intimacy. Instead, I settled against him, feeling the warmth of his body dry my wet cheek. Slowly my drained emotions re-charged and the silence became electric. It was then that Henry helped me relax into the most glorious sensations. It felt quite natural, somehow not unexpected, surprisingly not shocking. Afterwards he led me to his bed and eventually we slept. My dreams were far from peaceful.

*

Last summer was crap. On so many fronts. It had been obvious for some months that Oma was failing and the call from Pappi confirmed it.

'Benjamin, will you have the chance to get over to Vienna very soon?' My father's voice, still with its strong Austrian accent, reached down the phone as I sat in my usual spot in my usual bar, eating my usual pizza ahead of the last concert of the season.

When did we stop speaking to each other in German? It became the house rule to speak only English when we first arrived to live in the UK, but it was a strain and, for many years, he and I lapsed back into German whenever we were alone. Now it was only during visits to Austria that the German came to the fore.

'Has Tante Luisa phoned? Is Oma much worse?' The regular bulletin from Pappi's sister determined our family's mood as Oma swung from good days to bad.

'I'm travelling out in two days' time and I shall probably stay on until ...' He paused, recovered and added: 'She is being moved into a sanatorium tomorrow, where they can give her proper nursing. Luisa sounds very relieved that she won't have to cope alone anymore.'

'Both will be glad to see you,' I responded. 'Look, tonight is our last concert. I need to sort out some stuff so by Monday I should be able to follow you. I can stay as long as you need.'

I came off the phone, thoughts streaming into each other, and quickly phoned the news through to Georgie. The next day was Friday and, as already planned, my last chance to see her before Jeremy and Mark returned home for their frustratingly long summer holidays. I felt my longing for her stir.

Reaching Greystones for ten o'clock, I walked in, violin case in hand and a bag of music over my shoulder, the ostensible reason for my presence there. I placed both by the hall table and took Georgie in my arms. She pushed me back gently.

'I am so very sorry about your grandmother,' she said with a soft smile. 'You need to go to her, but I shall miss you dreadfully.'

'In some ways it will be easier for me to be right away from here. I'm not sure how I would handle real coaching sessions for Jeremy with you in the same room. I can pretend when we're in public, whereas here, where we have history …'

Georgie smiled and nodded before pulling me close again. I felt her body arch against me as she shuddered in anticipation of the coming sex. She took my hand and together we walked up the broad staircase along the familiar path to our room.

The room breathed Georgie. Over the months since I first followed her upstairs she had softened what was essentially a large study with a double bed in the corner. A thin sheet of blond wood rested on trestles, forming her desk beneath a wide window that gave out onto the mature trees of the back garden. The surface was covered neatly with her laptop, printer, stationery and piles of books. Many of them were in French, both hard-backs and well-worn paper-backs, and there was a huge French dictionary acting as bookend.

From the first this was the room where we had sex. I've never seen her bedroom, well, hers and Richard's. Nor did I wish to. Is there a contradiction in values that I could enter a man's wife but not his bed?

That day the first sex was fast and selfish, both of us taking from the other. After our urgency was sated, we lay close, fingers softly exploring until our bodies would again demand more urgent caresses. We talked of my departure.

'Will it be safe for me to send you texts?' I nuzzled her glorious chestnut brown hair.

'Yes. I'll keep my mobile on silent so that I can check calls without raising any curiosity and your number is plumbed in under a woman's name. My parents only ever call on the house phone; Richard calls my mobile; only the boys text me. I'll not let it out of my sight.'

'You can phone me any time,' I responded. 'Nobody in Austria will know who's calling me.'

'Yes, although I have to be careful in case Richard's book-keeper scrutinises my phone bill. His company pays all our mobile accounts.'

Those precious hours were memorable, not just because of the coming separation, but also because later I believed that they were our last together. At the time though, as we lay, sweat cooling our bodies in the growing heat of the day, we exhilarated in the moment. Her nakedness excited me as ever and my fingertips fluttered lightly over her skin. She shivered with pleasure. For a while something had puzzled me and now I dared to seek an answer. With my index finger I gently traced the barely visible scar above her luxuriant bush of soft brown curls.

'Was this an appendix?' I asked, realising full well that it wasn't.

'No.'

I felt her body tense beside me and I drew back to seek an explanation. Her eyes flickered briefly to mine then away, staring out of the window. It was always one of the good moments after sex with Georgie, just to lie side-by-side, our bodies scarcely touching, and see beyond the panes of glass to the branches of a massive beech tree. The restless leaves created a shimmering green patchwork against the blue sky.

I waited.

'I really don't want to talk about it.'

The tone of her response was unambiguous. *Don't go there.*

I wanted to probe further, instead I moved my hand to stroke her cheek, her lips, her nose, but our moment was lost and Georgina gave me a weak smile as she rolled away to her side of the bed and reached for her chocolate brown silk robe, discarded on the floor. I slid towards her and ran my fingertips from the nape of her neck down her spine. She twisted towards me.

'Look, I'm sorry, today's going to be frantic, and Mrs Bates will be round quite soon to clean the place before the boys arrive. I've already delayed her because of my 'music lesson' ...' Her voice trailed off and she stood abruptly to tie the belt of her robe. 'I lost a baby before Mark was born, but I really, really don't want to discuss it, OK?'

I nodded and turned away to dress. Not the ending I'd hope for ahead of a long separation. She slipped away while I pulled on my jeans and shirt. I met her standing at the bottom of the stairs, my music and violin cases in her hands.

'Sorry, that all came out wrong,' she said, passing them to me. I shook my head and shrugged. What do you say? Other than some crass comment. What do I know about having children, losing children? Though I was about to lose someone that I loved deeply, Oma.

'The summer will soon pass,' I said without great conviction. 'I'll be thinking about you all the time and I'll text you every day. You call me when you can.' Christ, that sounded hollow. 'Love you.' She smiled and I kissed her gently on the lips, breathing in her scent. She didn't stay to wave me off and the door closed behind me.

*

Georgie's devastating call came when I was already at my lowest ebb. We'd buried Oma a week earlier and the painful job of sorting through her stuff was getting to me, let alone my father and aunt. I wanted to escape back to

England. Just to see Georgie, even in the company of others, would be enough. I hated my need for her. Weakness.

The night before her call, my dreams had been confused and in the early hours I woke myself, crying out dry-mouthed, soundlessly. The words wouldn't come, no matter how hard I tried to shout. Exhausted, next morning I slept on until after nine when my mobile rang. In my muddled state, I scrabbled for the phone but it slid from my hand and, before I could answer, it switched to voicemail.

'Shit.' I checked the missed calls and saw it was Georgie. It had been over a week since she last phoned me and her text responses had been uncharacteristically brief. I'd been somewhat narked, however too wrapped up in what was going down in Vienna to focus on it.

As agreed, I couldn't return the call but must wait for her to finish the voicemail message and for it to be despatched through the ether, always an age when you're abroad. Finally a tone announced its arrival. With warm anticipation, I lay back onto my pillow to luxuriate in the sound of her voice. I always retained her recorded messages, only deleting the lesser ones as the mailbox became full.

'Benjamin,' her voice sounded hesitant. Instinctively I tensed. Then the message tumbled out.

'This is a dreadful time for you and I'm really sorry for this. I wanted to speak to you, not leave a message, instead I have to tell you now, while I have the courage.'

My body shut down.

'We have to stop this, this ...' Her voice hesitated. I knew the missing word.

'I've thought about it long and hard. I've had so much to consider in the last few days. There's no other way of saying this. I just cannot do this to Richard and the boys. I have loved you so deeply over the last months and if it's painful now, it can only get much worse if we continue. I have to get out now. I'm hurting you and that's the last thing I want to do, but we have to stop seeing each other. It has to end ... this madness.' Her voice faltered. 'This wonderful madness.

'Please don't contact me. I'm going away for a few days with Richard. He's been very ill and needs a break.'

Fuck Richard was my instinctive response.

'Benjamin, I am so, so sorry. And thank you.'

The message ended. Save or Delete. Automatically I pressed Save. Not that I wanted to hear that message repeated. I stared up at the hotel ceiling, my eyes fixed on the small winking red light of the fire alarm system. Until I could see it no more as my eyes blurred with tears of anger.

'Bitch.'

*

I'd been home a couple of days and chose Ritzlaff's Bach *Partita* to help me wade through the chores of washing, opening post and shuffling bills. The phone rang. I was cynical enough not to expect it to be Georgie. The orchestra manager spoke down the line and I turned down my music.

'Hi Benjamin.' His voice sounded softer than usual. 'How was it in Vienna? Sorry to hear about your grandmother.' I responded appropriately and waited to hear the real purpose of his call.

'Got some bad news, I'm afraid. Had a call last week from Georgina and poor old Richard's had some sort of a heart attack. A small one, fortunately, and he's going to be OK, they reckon.'

I was stunned for a moment and he took my silence for concern but I honestly didn't know what to say to him. My words croaked out: 'When did it happen? Was he at home?'

'About ten days ago. It happened while he was at work, I think. The paramedics got him to hospital in time and they were able to sort him out quickly. He's back home again, I hear. Just thought that, as they're your sponsors, you'd like to send them a note.'

Finishing the call I turned up the music again, but louder. I gazed out of the window to the red brick walls and grey slate roofs of the terraced houses opposite. My thoughts flew at me from all quarters. My concern for Richard was fleeting. He had survived. What if he hadn't? At once I saw plainly the fall-out from Georgie's phone message. Any hope of getting back together again had just evaporated. I sat at my table and with my two palms slowly beat out a drum riff which grew louder and faster.

*

Mahler's imperial theme continues at a more stately pace. Benjamin's arm tenses into a veritable piston as the violinists race against the woodwind and brass. He relaxes while, against drum rolls, cymbals and a lone horn in the distance, the melody subsides once more into chuckles. He lowers his bow. The movement settles softly towards silence as the cellos and basses opposite him pluck two final notes echoed by a single determined drum beat of warning.

He fears Jeremy has discovered his mother's secret.

Chapter Nine – Jeremy's Story

Jeremy strives to maintain his composure. He forces his attention away from his parents back to the music. Instinctively he identifies with the violinists as they hurtle into the second movement. His hands flex unconsciously in sympathy with the players' vigorous fingering. As brass and timpani probe ever further into the emotion of the music, he observes Benny's face fixed in concentration. Jeremy's jaw hardens.

At the crash of the cymbals, the girl beside him starts with surprise and shifts in her seat, crossing her bare legs. A wavering foot, encased in a nude-pink high-heel shoe, challenges his space.

*

Something definitely happened that evening, the first time I met Benny. Something passed between us. I'm sure it did. He really seemed genuinely interested in me. How fucking naïve was I? More likely he was just being polite to his sponsors. Or was it simply part of his plan to get closer to Mum?

Were they having it off even then? Whose idea was it to start the coaching sessions at home? Whatever, it was me who had the idea that she should join in on piano. And I just didn't get it. Not for one single moment.

Maybe the affair began after I returned to uni. That's probably when he started screwing her. All through that summer term, up 'til now. Except they can't have been at it during last year's summer holidays. Benny was in Austria then. And that's when Dad was taken ill. Christ, was she off shagging him all the time that Dad was convalescing?

*

Jeremy's train of thought is broken as the woodwind break into chuckles, one of his favourite passages, and he softens momentarily at Mahler's humour. The music relaxes further into an ethereal waltz, reminiscent of the heady times of by-gone Vienna, and he reflects on the great times with Benny.

*

We hit it off from the beginning. Benny is really easy to be around. As for my playing, he knew how to big me up, give me confidence.

'Look Jeremy, you've potential and I'm happy to help you get on, if you're prepared to put the time in. You OK with that?' Like a shot. Nobody had ever encouraged me like that. Except for Mum, but that's just what mothers say.

Dad seemed happy to pay for extra coaching and although initially Benny was embarrassed to take the money, Dad made the valid point to both of us that it would devalue Benny's position as a musician if he did not accept it. How ironical. I wonder if she continued to pay him for 'coaching' when I wasn't there?

From that first session, I learned that patience wasn't Benny's thing, but I accepted his criticism. Focused my mind. That was one advantage of Mum joining in; Benny had to curb that impatience. And there's no doubt about it, he is a good teacher. Whatever else he's done to my life, he's shaped my technique.

With the Easter holidays over, I returned to Birmingham. I was sorry our trio sessions had ended. It wasn't just that I'd learned a lot; it was awesome getting to know Benny and I didn't want to lose that contact. Back at uni, I kept in touch with him through email and Facebook. Well, actually, he accessed my Facebook page though never posted anything about himself. I should have guessed then that he had things to hide. Just thought he was a private sort of guy. He would read about what we'd covered in lectures then send a brief email with some ideas. It felt good to have someone watch out for me, someone who understood the music. Cared. So I was pretty hacked off when Dad mentioned in one of his emails that Benny continued to come over to the house to coach Mum. Benny had said nothing. Nor had Mum.

As the end of the summer term neared, I called him.

'Any chance we could get a couple of sessions in before you head for Austria? I've found a summer job in the village but it's only part-time.'

'Sorry mate,' was his swift response. 'I'm not going to be around. Probably need to go to Vienna earlier than planned. My grandmother isn't looking good. Catch up before the beginning of next term?' More a statement of fact than a suggestion. It would be months before I would see him again and I felt surprisingly flat at the prospect. Maybe he was regretting already his offer to coach me.

Home for the summer, I slipped back into family routine. There was a new tension though. Somehow, whenever I attempted to talk about Benny, Mum channelled conversation elsewhere. At the time I wondered if she had lost her passion for the piano and was finding the coaching a chore. More likely she'd transferred her passion elsewhere and wanted to draw us off the trail.

Was there an atmosphere last summer simply because we didn't get away on holiday? I was intent on earning as much as possible and couldn't afford a trip with mates from uni. When Dad announced that we wouldn't be going to Normandy, always the default destination when nothing else was on offer, I felt quite relieved. Holidays there held mixed recollections, some good, especially if Mima was with us, also some less so, when tension grew between Mum and Dad. Mark spoke for both of us, honestly, if bluntly.

'Whatever. We're past that sort of holiday now. Playing 'happy families'. Why don't you and Mum go off on your own? And I don't mean together.' He shrugged out of the room without waiting for a response. Surprisingly, Mum said nothing and turned away to clear the supper things, her mouth set in a mirthless smile.

It was best to ignore Mark. He was going through the *I think you're all crap* stage, preferring to burrow in his bedroom rather than mix with the rest of us. Though he never turned down the chance to earn holiday money by helping Dad's book-keeper with the business accounts. He would travel into the office with Dad, slumped into the passenger seat, headphones clamped to his ears, eyes shut. Dad complained it was like driving a zombie.

My attempts to keep in touch with Benny while he was in Vienna were none too successful. I'd send him texts though he was never forthcoming in his replies. My frustration switched to nagging anxiety and contact sort of tailed off but I couldn't get him out of my head. Had I done, said something to upset him?

*

It was October when I spotted the Simon Rattle concert coming to Birmingham. I hesitated, conscious of the months of little contact, then texted Benny. I knew he admired Rattle hugely and that he would jump at the chance of hearing the maestro in action.

Benny phoned back immediately. 'Hi mate, how's it going down in Brum?' I was encouraged.

'Good, just good. You?'

'Oh, you know, OK.' He sounded tired. 'I suppose I'm taking longer than I anticipated to get over my grandmother. She was old and it was expected, still …'

'Just thought that if you're not playing that night, you could come down and watch Rattle conduct. I need to get tickets soon as they're going fast, the usual thing when he returns to Birmingham.'

'Yes, go for it. I'll be free that night and I can get back here next day in time for rehearsals in the afternoon. I'll stay the night at my parents'.'

So, that's how it began. There was a crowd of us with students' tickets for the concert and I got Benny in on one of those. We met in the pub across the canal from the concert hall and I introduced him to my mates, all studying music. He was polite but I sensed that he was not totally at ease, irritated either by them or by something else. I couldn't tell. Amidst the thrum of voices, I asked if he'd seen anything of Mum and Dad now that my father was improved and back at work almost full-time. He said that he'd seen them at a recent sponsors' event but didn't expand on it. I pushed further and asked if he and Mum had picked up on their sessions. He dismissed that with a shrug. I took that for a 'no' and didn't pursue it. I was sort of pleased that they didn't meet up without me. Now I wonder what lay behind that shrug. Were they meeting but not admitting it?

At the end of the evening the audience went mad with applause and the hall zinged with hero worship. As Rattle returned for his third bow, I felt life couldn't get better than this. I turned to Benny and threw my arm around his shoulder. Bold? Scarily so. It just happened.

'Awesome! What a sound. Great you could be here with me.' He raised his hand to cover mine, still resting on his shoulder. Above the applause of the crowd I could just distinguish, 'Thanks, mate, good to be with you.' He squeezed my hand warmly. Yes!

The evening ended as Benny left to catch a bus to his parents' home. I walked with him to his stop on Broad Street and waited until the bus arrived, somehow wanting to prolong our time together.

'You must come down again soon, Benny. Just check the programme and tell me when you can make it. I know you like to see your folks ...' I hesitated, hardly daring to make the suggestion. 'Though if you prefer, why not crash down at mine? It'd be easier for you to get the train back north early the next morning.' My audacity scared me. His touch to my hand earlier; had it been a signal? I wasn't sure. I wanted it to be. He didn't seem to have girlfriends. Perhaps ...

In the garish light of that street, thronged as ever with people, young and middle-aged, all intent on a good night out, Benny looked at me, his eyes searching my face, my hair. I felt a blush claiming my neck when he replied.

'Why not, why not? I'd really like that.' He spoke earnestly, without a smile.

His bus arrived and, with a brief man hug, he was gone. I walked towards my own bus-stop with a feeling of elation, partly due to the concert, partly from a disturbing sense of anticipation.

*

I could never work out who was gay and who wasn't. At school it was really difficult to tell. There were some guys who dabbled in it, out of curiosity, and went straight for the rest of their lives. There were those who suspected they were gay and feared both that and discovery. They suppressed their inclinations and were miserable. Finally there were those who were straight but took malicious pleasure in trying to seduce virgin gays before subjecting them to painful and humiliating exposure. Which is why I've always held back from coming out to friends or the family. Especially my family. I always thought Mum might understand. Dad? No way. And Mark?

Things were sort of OK between me and Mark throughout our childhood. We weren't exactly best mates, though nor did we fight particularly. He was self-sufficient, even from a toddler. Maybe that's a trait of the second child, wanting to demonstrate their own ability, independent of the older sibling.

Although we overlapped at boarding school by only a couple of years, we had nothing to do with each other, simply because that's how it was; you didn't mix with younger years. It was when I went up to uni that I saw a hardening in him; perhaps that's part of being a teenager. During holidays, when we were both at home, he could be a total prat, giving us all grief with his moodiness.

By last Christmas, I reckon that Mark had discovered somehow that Benny was screwing around with Mum. When, how did he find out? Why didn't the little tosser tell me? Probably got a kick out of knowing something I didn't.

Then this January, when Benny turned down the Gergiev concert. I bet it was because of her. She made him a better offer. A better fuck than me.

Is this what life is? You fall for someone, open up to them, trust them. Then zap! Right between the eyes. Loser.

Last autumn I'd never been so happy. For the first time I could be myself; at least, not pretend that I was something that I could never be. Everything in life buzzed – uni, my music, all because of Benny. I was comfortable with our secret.

True, we didn't get to meet up that often and there was only that one time that he stayed over and we ...

Benny was always guarded in any exchanges of text or email. I understood. Nevertheless, I read rejection into every unreturned message. I couldn't help myself.

Discretion mattered to me too. I wasn't ready to tell Mum and Dad. Mark? Maybe he already guessed I was gay, but I felt sure he'd be cool with the whole thing. Perhaps he'd even support me when I eventually came out.

Benny didn't want people to find out that he was gay, even within his artistic world. Nobody would have batted an eyelid, but he wanted to conceal our relationship. Misguidedly, I thought he was sensitive that his sponsors may not be comfortable with us being an item, especially Dad. All the time it was really to prevent Mum finding out. How fucking ironic.

To be honest, at the time it was enough for me that I'd found Benny. Someone who wanted me just as much as I longed for him. So I thought.

The approaching Christmas holidays were always going to be tricky because all three of us would be too busy for our coaching session. I phoned Benny.

'So, we can't meet up, just the two of us?' I ventured.

'Sorry mate, won't be possible. It's all-out rehearsal, then concert after concert. You know what it's like; we have to ram them in for the popular Christmas stuff to make money when we can.'

'I could possibly come over to your place, if you like?'

'No way,' was his disappointingly brusque response. 'Place is a tip and I need space to practise then sort myself out to head home to the folks. It's our first Christmas since Oma died, and being Jewish doesn't change the sentiment of the season.' Not at all what I wanted to hear. So, I would head north for the holiday just as he travelled south to the Midlands and his family. In my insecurity I worried that he wanted out. I couldn't let that happen.

'We can at least say hello at the concert on the twenty-third,' was my positive response.

In the event, I did see Benjamin at the pre-Christmas concert, but it wasn't what I'd hoped for. We always took Nanna and Grandad for their annual spot of culture. Mum had dropped out, claiming last minute late-night shopping, and Mark was forced to take her ticket, to the delight of our grandparents.

During the interval, the players, dressed festively in white tuxedos, came into the foyer to wish their sponsors a happy Christmas. Benny was edgy. Did he feel between us the same electricity that zinged through me? We greeted with a casual arm around the shoulder. Touching him, even in public, was stimulating. But he pulled away quickly and faced Mark, preparing to give a blokey grab of his left shoulder. Mark pulled back and deflected Benny's hand, walking off with a scowl. Dad, busy getting drinks for Nanna and Grandad, hadn't noticed Mark's arsy behaviour. Benny gave a brief shrug and turned to my grandmother with a fixed smile.

'Sorry about that, Benny,' I apologised, mortified by Mark's reaction. 'What was that all about?' In mitigation I reached out a hand to touch his arm but he withdrew it with a scarcely concealed glare. I felt like a child slapped by a favourite uncle.

During the concert, as I gazed down on him, the hurt soon dissipated. His wiry body responded to the demands of the score, now gently swaying with a lilting childhood carol, now vigorously bowing with the beat of a seasonal pop song orchestrated for symphonic sound. We had to tread carefully, I knew that. Our secret was wonderful and precious. Naïve or what?

*

Jeremy looks across to his parents and from their body language he spots that something is wrong. His father is looking down into his lap. From where Jeremy sits, slightly lower than the ledge, he cannot see more but guesses from the undisguised fury on his mother's face that his father has opened a message on his phone.

That's not like Dad, not in a concert. He frowns. *Something to do with the deal? Mum will go ape.* He is conscious that the girl on his left is also looking in that direction.

Shit, everyone can see what he's up to. How could his father be so gross? The girl, sensing his eyes on her, glances back at him and he recognises something familiar in her face. Who is she?

The muted notes of the brass lead to affirming *pizzicato* from cellos and basses and the drum beat brings the movement to a defined end. In the pause between movements, Jeremy looks again at his mother. She had been the one he trusted, the one who last weekend held him close as he admitted that he was gay and declared his love of Benny. The last person on earth who would betray him.

His mother faces his father. His father looks out across the hall, no doubt considering the message he has just read.

Chapter Ten – The Girl's Story

The viciousness of the opening bars matches the girl's fury at seeing the woman. She watches the scurrying elbows of the string players and feels that same energy pent up inside her. Despite the sounds flying up from all sections of the orchestra, she jumps when a musician below her clashes a pair of cymbals. Irritated at being startled, she crosses one fake-tanned leg over the other and senses that the guy beside her disapproves. She sits back to observe him out of the corner of her eye. She sees an earnest face, slightly frowning.

Her attention returns to the arms thrashing below her. Energetic stuff. Calm returns and she observes the slowly rocking backs of the musicians who now play more floaty music on flutes and stuff.

She eyes the woman once more.

*

Mum has always grafted. Still does. When I was a kid, she worked long hours. She was the breadwinner and had no other choice. She was always there for me, though. Even after I was old enough for a front door key, she did her best not to be home late. There was always a meal of sorts and afterwards I'd be expected to clear away, 'do pots' and get things ready for next morning's breakfast grab. While I was tatting about she would sit at the table, Walkman fixed to her ears as she got down to her paperwork. I toyed with my homework then slumped in front of the box before being ordered to bed around ten. She continued working.

She's a bloody good saleswoman and loves to do a deal. The Bear always encouraged her and acted as a sounding board whenever she reached a crossroads in her career. Like the time when I was studying for my A levels. He came round early, shovelled down a Tesco's lasagne without noticing it, then cleared the decks to open one of his black A4 notebooks and, Mont Blanc pen poised, waited for my mother to lay out her plan.

'I don't know how much longer I'll have the energy to continue like this.' She lit a cigarette, despite his distaste for smoking. I wondered how he could bear to kiss someone who smoked. 'Selling is a young person's game and I need to find something where I can still use these skills, but not at this pace.' She outlined her thoughts of setting up a recruitment business, specialising in medical sales.

'Yeah, yeah, you've talked about that before.' He didn't try to conceal his impatience. 'So prove to me why you think you could make a go of it.' In the ensuing to-and-fro, Mum flagged her strengths. He put up loads of obstacles, to make sure she'd thought things through. It was the right step for her and he knew it. Since then she's not looked back. Not only does she earn more, she's a recognised success. It's not been easy, but my Mum doesn't do 'easy'.

*

So now, let's see, where are you sitting? I bought you a ticket for the top tier, neatly out of sight.

I feel really high tonight. A mixture of butterflies and adrenalin. It'll be a catharsis. Catharsis. I like that word. Heard it on a TV debate and looked it up: a purifying of the emotions brought about in the audience of a tragic drama through intense fear and pity. Forget the 'pity'.

*

When did I clock just how much The Bear manipulates Mum? Even now, I'm not sure she realises that he's still pulling her strings. It's cleverly done. Never through bullying, he's more Machiavellian than that. A subtle suggestion here, a 'what if' there, and because it comes from him, the seed is sown on fertile ground and so flourishes into an idea that has just occurred to my mother. Clever, or what?

He got involved whenever she needed to deal with my Dad's solicitors. Despite being a good saleswoman always up for bargaining, when it came to her own situation, Mum lost her nerve. Ahead of discussions for a hike in my maintenance, The Bear would prime her, checking what she would write or say.

Some six months ahead of my eighteenth birthday, things became tense between the two of them. Although she preferred to keep me out of their discussions, this time I insisted. After all, I knew that from now on my father had no legal obligation to continue payments.

'I want to go to uni. So why shouldn't he continue to fork out?' I demanded one evening as we all sat around the table, cleared plates pushed to one side.

'You can't let him stop now,' The Bear exploded as Mum protested that I was legally an adult and her new business wasn't doing too badly. 'You're missing the bloody point. She's about to go to university and that'll cost you big time. You're earning too much to get a grant so get the bugger to contribute. You can bet your life that his kids will go to university. They're probably at some posh public school as we speak.'

He knew how to put the knife in.

'Maybe eighteen years ago you made the wrong decision, Mum?' The spite in my voice was unjust but I felt aggrieved as much against her as that man. 'I bet you could have had him in the end. Why did you give up and let him go?'

The Bear sat silently and watched. My mother flushed with anger and turned on me.

'You have no idea what you're talking about. No way did I want him. I handled things in absolutely the right way. I've worked bloody hard for you, madam, without having to sacrifice myself for the sake of some man who just wanted a good shag on the side.'

I was shocked into silence. Was that it? Was I the outcome of a 'good shag on the side'?

The Bear intervened. 'For fuck's sake shut up, the both of you. This isn't getting us anywhere. The crucial thing is to get him to stump up for your fees. End of.'

'We have no legal claim once she's eighteen,' countered my mother. 'And don't forget, he's paid up regularly as clockwork, even before the Child Support Agency existed.'

'Why are you defending him?' The Bear sat back exasperated. 'He only did that to keep the whole thing secret from his wife.' He glanced quickly at me, checking my reaction.

'And that's why he'll want to continue supporting me through uni,' I smiled. 'Last thing he wants is for an eighteen year-old secret turning up on his wife's doorstep. We need to think this through. I'm interested in more than the money now.' Across the table, Mum frowned her unspoken question.

'Don't you both see? Of course he'll pay up because he's frightened you'll tell his wife. What I want is to make him feel bad, really bad. Guilty as hell. Not for cheating on his wife or whatever she was then, but for cheating on me. Thinking he could simply pay me off and cut me out of his life for eighteen years. We've got to find something that turns the screws, something that money won't buy off.'

It was The Bear who came up with the solution. At first Mum was horrified, it was going too far, but I saw that it could work. Make the bastard feel guilty as well as ensure I got my uni paid for. Yeh, I owe The Bear, though at the time I didn't understand why he was so keen to get one over that man, other than on my account. Was there something from the past, something so big that The Bear wanted so badly to screw him over?

In demanding that extra support, Mum's threats were veiled. After all, it's a fine line between chancing your arm and out and out blackmail. The message landed and after the solicitor received the evidence my father demanded, a significant hike in my payments was confirmed on the understanding that they would stop after my years at university. How did The Bear get hold of that proof? Surely not legally? What straight doctor would fabricate that sort of documentation?

*

Oblivious to the music, the girl gazes over the audience and notices a middle-aged couple at the edge of the hall on the ground floor. She watches the woman, encased in a wheelchair, and the man beside her, resting his hand on one of its arms. Both are totally wrapped up in the music, for the moment transported out of their situation. For a nanosecond she feels a stab of shame that she, too, is supposed to be wheelchair-bound.

*

It certainly wouldn't have been easy at uni, getting around in a wheelchair. Possible, though not easy. And I certainly wouldn't have come up on Ned's radar. I had no illusions about what he was after. I am what I am: middling fit and not bad looking. 'She scrubs up well,' is how The Bear describes me.

Guys seem to like me, though before uni there was nobody serious when me and my friends hung out with some of the lads off the estate. After I started at Southampton, I hoped to find a different sort, someone to escape with. I chose my local uni because it would be cheaper to live at home. I'd have preferred to go to another part of the country but we couldn't afford it. That was that. I learned early on from Mum: don't moan, just get on with life.

I fancied Ned from the outset. We were both doing Marketing and were paired up for some seminars. He was a northerner from what Mum would call a 'good' family, but he was naughty. And I really like 'naughty'. Even though I guessed he was using me, I ended up prepping seminars for him too. Still, it worked both ways: I was also using him. He had plenty of money and would take me to parties and gigs that no way I could afford. He had a flat in the city, paid for by Mummy and Daddy of course. I would often overnight there, much to Mum's annoyance.

'Look, as long as I pass, get over it.'

In the end, my 2:1 more than satisfied her.

The relationship with Ned brought home to me that even if my background didn't matter to him, he mixed in different circles compared to the estate where I'd grown up, and the difference showed. The weekend Ned invited me to go 'up north' to stay with his family was not a good one. His parents were politely warm towards me. The Saturday night spent with his mates at the local pub was an eye-opener. His reputation as the local bad boy didn't come as a surprise to me and I sensed there was more than one girl in the room that he'd shagged, who didn't welcome this nobody from the South. One, Abi, big eyes and tits to match, could hardly bear to speak to me and, when she did, her coolness emerged as disdain.

'So, after you graduate, will your family be helping you find a position?'

'Hardly,' Ned interjected before I could speak. I shrugged and inspected the collection of brewery branded water jugs suspended from the ceiling. I curbed the anger towards Abi and more so towards Ned for highlighting my mongrel origins. Obviously, certain people believe that where you come from matters still. Surely, by now aren't there enough successful people in the world who can demonstrate it's all about you and what you can achieve for yourself?

As we drank, I searched my head for a come-back. *Condescending bitch.* But it was Ned's response that cut deeper.

The understated designer jacket on the back of Abi's chair gave me inspiration. We were seated inside the pub so a cigarette burn was a non-starter. Instead I drifted off to the Ladies where I carefully palmed an exposed lipstick. The group was beginning to break up and I hovered behind Abi's chair, speaking animatedly to Ned who responded likewise, drawing attention to himself. It was a matter of seconds to drag my hand and the hidden lipstick across the back of her jacket.

'It's been great to meet you all, good luck with the point-to-point,' to the rosy cheeked Young Farmer; 'Enjoy music college,' to the Aspiring Violinist. I leant forwards and with my free hand, patted Abi's shoulder. 'And such fun to meet you, too, Abi.' Then we were gone.

Maybe it was the focus of exams that did for us. No way was I going to piss around like Ned ahead of our finals. Revision was revision. On the day exams ended, there was a distinct cooling on his side as we all drank ourselves stupid. Was he crapping himself with the realisation that he'd blown it? Whatever, after he returned north, following a few calls, then texts, it petered into nothing. Was I gutted? Sort of, but he wasn't what I was looking for. Even now, I'm not sure I know what I want.

What do I need in a guy? Perhaps it all gets mixed up in what I once sought in a Dad. He'd be tall, have a sense of humour, an easy smile, look good in casual clothes, especially tight jeans. He'd be active. As a kid, I always wanted a Dad to play ball with me on the beach. He'd take me horse riding and show me how to snorkel. And he'd ruffle Mum's hair to annoy her, only because he loved her. What total crap. Life's not like that.

Love just isn't like that either. Cynical or what, I don't see how love can last. Duty, responsibility, affection, perhaps yes. Maybe that's the best it gets. Take The Bear: no idea how many years he was married and he stuck with her to the end, the bitter end. Breast cancer, poor woman. Must be four years ago now. Did she guess he was two-timing her with Mum all those years when I was growing up? Maybe what you don't know can't hurt. Who's to say? For sure, nobody should judge until they're in the same place?

After his wife's death, The Bear didn't come to see us for some months. Was it guilt? Was he really grieving?

When he called again, he appeared no different than before and invited Mum to go away with him for a week in Portugal. I looked forward to their return with expectation.

'Fantastic,' was Mum's response to my questioning as I made her a cup of tea. 'Lovely place, weather, just great.'

'And how did you both get on? Was it different this time, um, since …?'

She put her mug down and her tanned face became strained. 'I know what you're fishing for, but no, we're not getting together. It's never been on the agenda, so just forget it.' Was she tired from the journey, or just resigned? Was it her dream to live with him, maybe even to marry him? I'm not certain, though I suspect that it was. Maybe dreams are best kept as dreams in case they fail the reality test.

*

The music goes berserk, the brass players giving their all with some sort of fanfare. The girl feels exhilarated and flexes her painted fingers. Her eyes again search the audience, trying to distinguish The Bear among the packed seats high at the back of the hall, the only discreet place she could get a ticket for him. Even if she cannot spot him, he can probably pick out her distinctive pink dress as she sits exposed, high behind the orchestra. Has he sent the text yet? So far, she has spotted no reaction from the man on the ledge.

At the height of what she hears as chaos, a musician close below her whacks a gong and the music subsides into a chattering exchange. Now she sees the man, head bowed, looking at something glowing on his lap. *Yes!* He straightens up, his face averted from the orchestra. The girl cannot gauge his reaction. She sees the woman turn to him and the girl imagines her disapproval.

As the music closes with a mournful sign-off from the tuba and a gentle drum-beat, the girl smiles. *That's pushed a spike up your arse, just like my voice-mail this afternoon.*

Aware of the guy on her right, she looks at him and meets his puzzled eyes. *What's with you, dude?*

THIRD MOVEMENT *Scherzo*

Chapter Eleven – Richard's Story

French horns open the witty third movement. Wind instruments enter, followed by the strings in an optimistic dance. Richard observes the clarinet players thrust their instruments high in loud celebration but shares none of their sentiment. The ensuing edgy discord resonates better with his own tumult as he struggles to fight down panic, to think logically. The message is from Mulligan, starkly setting out the new rules of engagement.

Saddlethwaite Councils CEO meets me tomorrow at 2. Will share my concerns re serious breach of ethics. So just tomorrow am to close the deal. Am sure you agree its imperative for deal to conclude as proposed.

His face burns with helpless anger. Georgina continues to glare at him, her hands clenched.

*

It's a bluff. It's got to be. I was so careful; nothing in writing to trace that weekend back to me or Ian. Other than the hotel register, and I bet Ian didn't write down Tracy's real name. I paid for both rooms with cash, so no evidence there. For God's sake, Ian wouldn't have disclosed anything in case it got back to his wife.

But Mulligan doesn't fly kites. So that's it, he's got something on me. If he's prepared to take it to Saddlethwaite and go public, I'm fucked. Well and truly fucked. No way can I stop him getting the business now.

*

The music descends into a wrangle between threatening brass and a single French horn. Richard shifts in his seat, feels over-heated and longs to slip out of his jacket.

When the news gets out that his business has collapsed, how many will recall seeing him at tonight's concert? And remember that he appeared stressed. He looks over to the lawyer opposite. *You won't be inviting us round for the summer barbecue this year.* As the strings pizzicato a melody reminiscent of eastern Europe, Richard gazes over the players below but sees nothing.

*

What was it that Mulligan said to his PA this afternoon? Throughout the meeting, she sat impassively at his side, saying nothing, taking occasional notes.

'Sarah, be a doll, and confirm my meeting tomorrow afternoon. Might as well cram in as much as possible while I'm up here.' He turned to me with a smile that never reached his eyes. 'We should be done by lunch-time tomorrow, don't you think, Rich?'

Sarah snatched a quick glance in my direction then nodded to him without any discernible expression. She must have been aware of what Mulligan was planning.

If I don't agree to his terms tomorrow morning, Mulligan will go to Saddlethwaite Council and expose Ian for taking a bribe. A weekend in Sussex hardly constitutes a bribe, for fuck's sake, but that's not how their compliance people would see it, nor the press, nor Ian's wife. Christ, he'd get the boot and I'd be totally stuffed. Mulligan is on track to get my business for a song and there's no time to set up my exit plan.

What to tell Georgina? The house will have to go. No way on Mulligan's terms can I manage the mortgage and this time her father won't cough up to help us through. He was never that happy about paying the boys' school fees. Ironic really that the pressure to do so came from Georgina's mother. So much for French *égalité*. How will Georgina react? She'll be mortified but, without question, she won't go flaky. She'll probably even offer to get a job. Georgina's good in a crisis. Like when I was ill. Solid as a rock.

Down-size, that's what we'll do, even though it'll break her heart to leave Greystones. So many happy memories, even in this short time. That kitchen is her real pride and joy. She's happiest presiding over the kitchen table with her three 'boys' tucking into her mother's recipe for beef stew, or *daube* as she calls it.

Georgina revels in entertaining, whether casually in the kitchen for our friends, or more formally in the dining room where the high ceiling and oak panels never cease to impress. I watch clients as we walk them into dinner, especially in winter when the midnight blue velvet curtains are drawn against the night and the table is lit by candles reflecting off the china and crystal. Some take it all in and choose not to comment, others are immediate and fulsome in their admiration.

'What a smashin' place you've got here, Richard. So that's where our fees go, then?' joked the leader of Saddlethwaite council, half seriously, when we were close to winning the new industrial park by-pass.

Most elegant of all is our drawing room. We only use it for entertaining and at Christmas when the tree stands in the bay window, dressed in white and silver, an impressive sight as visitors approach up the drive. Pride of place goes to her baby grand. I love to watch her playing, back curved gently forwards, hands sinuously flowing across the keys. A pity she never got to play professionally. Kids put an end to that. Good that she's playing again now. Maybe she could teach piano, though I don't suppose that it would bring in much. Benjamin would tell her what her chances are. Ah, Benjamin. She won't be happy that we'll have to cut his sponsorship. And we won't be able to afford so many concerts either.

Jeremy finishes uni this term, so he'll have to get out into the jobs market and fend for himself. Probably won't be playing his fiddle though, unless he resorts to busking. It would be cheaper for him if he came back to live at home, though I doubt that he will. In my heart I feel he's left us for good already. I can't get close to him anymore. It's not about his music; it's much deeper than that. As though he's frightened of me. It started just after he went away to board.

Mum was really upset when he first went away to school.

'Poor lad, he's so young to be sent from home,' she said over Sunday lunch.

Jeremy wriggled uncomfortably in his seat, desperate for the subject to be dropped. We knew he wasn't totally enamoured at the prospect of sleeping in a dormitory, even if only with three other boys. She spotted my frown and held her peace. Later, when I drove her and Dad home, she continued:

'Mind he doesn't get in with the wrong sort. Even posh boys do drugs. We could lose him for ever.' I hoped that she would be wrong. Now I'm not sure. We haven't lost him to drugs, well, I don't think so, but I'm certainly not getting through to him.

As for Mark, I despair. A year ago I'd have said that we had a good thing going, even with him away at school. During the holidays we always did great stuff together, like golf, but in the last twelve months he's become a real dick; morose, uncommunicative, other than when he's giving his mother a hard time. There's no respect.

One Saturday during last year's summer holidays, I grabbed my moment. Jeremy was off somewhere and I waited for Georgina to pop into the village. I was feeling pretty run down and my patience was stretched. Mark was in his room, totally absorbed in some computer game.

'May I come in?' I asked as I walked into his domain. He grunted without turning towards me. I perched on his still un-made bed. 'Mark, would you mind switching that thing off for a minute? We need to talk.' I kept my voice light but the firmness was undisguised.

Mark grunted again, which I took for acquiescence, then a couple of minutes later closed down the game. He swivelled his chair and faced me unspeaking and with a blank expression which my Dad would have called 'dumb insolence'.

'Mark, I'm not happy with the way you talk to your mother. You're insolent and totally out of order. Whether it's teenage hormones or whatever, I will have you show respect to your mother. Do you understand?'

He started to speak, then shrugged and with hands resting on his knees, looked down at the carpet.

'Was that a 'sorry, OK' shrug or a 'whatever' shrug?' Nobody shrugs at me, especially not my son.

His face remained set.

'What's up, Mark? Why have you changed from a perfectly reasonable guy into some glowering prat that I don't recognise as my son? I thought you and I got on OK. I thought you were enjoying learning to play golf with me. Heaven knows I don't have much spare time but at least I make an effort for that. And I've found you a summer job in the company. It's only sorting invoices but you're getting paid for it.'

My raised voice took him aback and he looked straight at me, his face for the first time registering emotion, albeit an emotion that I couldn't read.

'Sorry Dad. I'm grateful for the job and the money. And for taking me to the driving range.' He swivelled his seat so that he looked out into the garden and his face was hidden.

'It's nothing to do with you, Dad, not really. With Mum, it's just ...' his head dropped again. '... difficult.'

'Yes, well, life is difficult, Mark, so for God's sake sort yourself out. I won't have you speaking to your mother like that. She doesn't deserve it. Do you understand?'

Mark turned back to face me as though to say something. He remained silently frowning. With that I stood up and picked my way out of the room. What was it he wanted to tell me?

If things improved between Mark and Georgina, it was only marginal and probably only furthered by my collapse soon after.

Georgina says that I gave too much time to the job and not enough to the boys when they were younger. Christ, how does she imagine we've been able to afford all this: holidays, great house, private schooling? The business doesn't just run itself, for fuck's sake. What more could I have done?

*

The sound gently builds before horns and trombones vie for supremacy. Trumpets and clarinets are played with vigour, held aloft. Georgina nudges Richard and frowns quizzically. He looks at her blankly. How can he tell her that he is about to fall out of his world, taking her with him? Instead he gives her a reassuring smile as the violins flow into the waltz-like theme that whirls breathlessly, with no escape.

*

My heart scare nearly a year ago was a real test for Georgina, for us all. Prompted by her father, now a retired GP, she came up with all manner of suggestions, many contrary to the advice from my specialist. It may have been fear, possibly my medication, but I found myself snapping at her. No wonder that with me and then Mark playing the bastard, she seemed to withdraw into herself towards the end of that summer.

Christmas was dire. We had her parents up to stay. On the day, my parents came over with my sister, Tricia, home from Geneva for the festivities. I thought that she of all people would cheer up Georgina, sharing gossip about life in Switzerland. Unfortunately, even that failed to raise a spark, quite the reverse.

For Christmas lunch we used the dining room with best china and tablecloth, an heirloom once belonging to Georgina's French grandmother. Despite all the ingredients of success - expensive wines to accompany the two geese, both Aga roasted to perfection - around that table of nine the only people unaware of the tension were my parents. Afterwards, as I was polishing the crystal glasses, my sister cornered me.

'So, how's the old heart now? Feeling back to normal again?'

'I'm great, thanks, never better,' was my standard response to such enquiries. Why tell people that actually I felt permanently knackered and things were more of an effort than ever before?

'Tell me, does the medication affect your sex drive?' I stopped polishing the glass in my hand, held it up to check for smears, then placed it carefully on a tray.

'Why do you ask? Should it?'

Tricia hesitated. 'There's something about you and Georgina, a distance. Thought you both might be frustrated?'

'Absolutely not, you cheeky cow,' I laughed perhaps too heartily. 'We'll have been married twenty-five years next year, so it's not every other night, but we don't do badly,' I lied. Was it the drugs, was it the fear engendered by the attack? Whatever, we hadn't had sex since. Did it show? I didn't miss it – too much else on my mind. What about Georgina? Did she need it?

It played on my mind. Was she happy? The last thing I needed was a dodgy marriage. I ought to make an effort. After all, she was still a looker and hadn't let her figure go.

Shortly after the boys went back for the spring term, I took her out to dinner, somewhere classy. I tried to find romantic things to say, even though it didn't come easily anymore, and Georgina looked uncomfortable. My intention to sweep her off her feet and make love when we got home petered out somewhere on the drive back and, as we lay in bed my half-hearted overtures were gently rebuffed, to my great relief. Women of a certain age, as the French generously describe middle-aged women, go through all sorts of hormonal change so I concluded that she'd gone off sex as much as I had.

*

Why in thinking of sex do I recall Melanie? Sex for her was natural, to be relished. Unsurprisingly, it's not often now that I remember her for the good times. Over the last twenty-six years she has proved to be a first-class bitch. I refuse to add up what it's cost me to pay for her daughter. Our daughter.

Would I have behaved similarly in her place? Was it instinct that drove her to protect the child, particularly when they diagnosed MS?

My solicitors contacted me with the news just before the girl's eighteenth birthday. I couldn't believe it. Surely, Melanie was trying it on. Strange coincidence that the girl had been diagnosed with MS just around the age when I would be no longer liable for Child Support.

'We should demand medical proof,' said the latest in a long series of young solicitors to care for my 'business' over the last eighteen years. Melanie's solicitor must have been expecting the challenge, as a signed medical note duly arrived. It confirmed that the girl was suffering from the unusually early stages of multiple sclerosis, listed how the condition affected her currently and outlined how her mobility would become increasingly impaired, eventually requiring a wheelchair.

'What are your instructions then, Richard?' asked my uninterested lawyer, Amanda or Samantha or some such. I'd been pondering my response in the intervening days, guessing that Melanie wouldn't chance her hand without a strong case. Providing more money would not be easy. There was no spare money but in the letter from Melanie's solicitors it was implicit that failure to cough up for the girl's university fees would lead eventually to disclosure of her existence to Georgina. And the world would come down like a pack of cards. No way would Georgina accept deception on that scale. As for her parents?

'Tell her yes,' was my reluctant response. How could I do otherwise?

Somehow I found the money, though it meant scuppering plans for two weeks in Portugal. Instead that summer we returned *en famille* to her parents' cottage in Normandy for the *n*th time. I told Georgina that I had cash flow problems so Portugal was no-go and together we agreed to tell the boys that Poppa wanted us to do some DIY at the cottage. I hated that place, where it was expected that I should pay for our holiday with lawn mowing and other jobs that seemed to take days to complete. Some bloody holiday.

Fortunately, business bucked up and I was just able to manage the payments. Now it's going to fall apart. If I agree to the deal with Mulligan, how would I finesse the money transfer through the company without him or Georgina finding out?

What about Melanie? If she gets stroppy, she might come looking for the money. If Georgina finds out, I'm shafted on all sides. No, Melanie will have to understand that, despite the MS, I can no longer pay. So there's nothing to be gained in blackmailing me.

Why the hell should I continue shelling out? Legally I no longer have any financial obligation. It's down to the State now. That's why I pay taxes. I'm not even sure that they still live in Southampton. All contact has been through the lawyers. Best that way. Keeps the emotion out of it. Surely, it was better for the girl that I kept out of her life? After all, that's what Melanie stipulated way back.

*

The solo horn offers its doleful voice towards the highest tier of the auditorium, then softens. The orchestra takes a deep breath before bullying forth, ganging up against the horn section until the movement ends on a triumphant flourish. Richard's collar is choking him and during the pause he loosens his lemon silk tie and undoes the top button of his blue striped shirt. He pushes his glasses up to the bridge of his nose, breathes deeply and ignores his wife's questioning eyes.

He is desperate to get an answer back to Mulligan.

Chapter Twelve – Georgina's Story

The insistence of the opening French horns draws Georgina back to the present and she glares at her husband. His face is flushed and perspiring. She clasps her hands tightly in helpless frustration.

What the hell's going on? She feels sick. *Has he found out? How? Has he bugged my study? A private investigator? What am I thinking? Of course not. Richard would never do that.*

Georgina's skin prickles. Since the affair resumed, she has taken the greatest care to be discreet.

To her ears, even the orchestra sounds out of kilter. The woodwind snigger, like gossips among the supermarket shelves.

*

The end of last year was horrendous. Autumn greyness coloured my mood as I mouldered in my study, watching dripping leaves tumble to the sodden earth. Where was I going with my life? I felt dreary, guilty not to be thankful for all I had. Richard hadn't died in the summer and was making great progress, though at times he was challenging to live with. Actually, he's even more challenging now. Perhaps that's down to his meds.

He noticed my constant edginess and patently had his own interpretation.

'Darling, you really aren't yourself these days. We all seem to be in your bad books. Maybe you should go and see the doc?' Christ. He thought I was going through the change. Bad move, Richard. My impassioned denial probably only served to confirm his suspicions but he apologised and retreated even further into his work. That worried me more, especially as Doc Whitehouse had told him repeatedly to slow down for the sake of his health.

I cast around for meaningful ways of spending my time. Yes, I had my music appreciation group but that would scarcely guarantee my sanity. My mother, who had always rejected the expected stereotype of the GP's wife by refusing to do any voluntary work, was less than helpful when I escaped down to stay with her for a brief visit.

'You have a brain, Georgina, use it. Study, research, write,' were her suggestions as she chopped vegetables for a casserole. 'What has happened with your music? Is that young violinist inspiring you still?' This with a quizzical smile. What did she mean by that? Did she suspect that I was having an affair? Is that what she expected, what she would have done? It shocked me to think that she might have been unfaithful to Papa.

Miserably I shrugged my shoulders.

'Christmas will soon be here. You and Papa are coming up to Greystones and on the day Richard's parents will come over with Tricia, too, so there'll be lots to do. I'll think about it in the New Year.'

'Ah yes, Tricia, is she still in Genève?' I nodded.

'She must be in her mid-fifties now? Is she still saving babies in Africa?'

'Maman, she's done really well and is now a director of the charity. I think you'll find that they do more than saving babies in Africa. The family is really proud of her.'

'That could have been you if you hadn't married and settled down with babies.' A pause while she tipped the wooden board and the roughly chopped celery and carrots cascaded into her beloved earthenware *marmite*. 'Do you regret the way your life has played, chèrie?' Maman had never believed that having babies was woman's destiny, despite the evidence of civilisation. It was a question I found difficult to answer at that moment. The emptiness of my life was stretching before me and I didn't want to acknowledge it, not to my smugly contained mother. I turned the question.

'Because it worked for Tricia doesn't mean it would have done so for me.' I reached to take the board and knife to wash, in doing so made eye-contact. 'What about you, Maman? Looking back on your life at seventy-five, what would you have done differently? Would you have married a Frenchman, for example?'

'No, there is much about my nation I dislike, though maybe if you had married a Frenchman there would have been more spirit in your life.'

That was the only time my mother ever expressed a criticism, implied or otherwise, of Richard. Prescient as ever, she spoke plainly at a time when I was shrieking inside with the futility of it all.

*

By Christmas, Richard was much stronger and we were back to our busy social diary with drinks parties, theatre and concerts woven into the demands of his business life. God I loathed the annual client entertaining. It wasn't the cost of wining and dining them, more the sheer boredom that got to me. Occasionally there would be a couple that talked beyond their children and their holidays.

For the orchestra patrons' pre-Christmas party, the sponsors sat with their particular player. I dreaded this confrontation with Benjamin, the first since we parted in early summer. The table plan had us sitting either side of him which meant I had another sponsor to my left. Did Richard notice the paucity of conversation between me and Benjamin? Possibly not as he was on good form and keen to talk about the overseas tour of the coming season. As Benjamin outlined the cities they would visit and the programmes that would be performed, I became heavily engrossed in conversation with an elderly lady who reminisced about concerts attended since childhood. Much of it I hardly heard, but I was able to lob the occasional question and she was off on a new tack. All the while, my other ear tuned into the quietly assertive voice I knew so well.

Christmas arrived in a blur of shopping, present wrapping, decorations, cooking, exhaustion. I was snappy with everyone, and made a massive effort to be pleasant before guests. Tricia was my only oasis when, on the afternoon of Christmas Eve, she joined me to peel and bag carrots and Brussels sprouts while I prepared the bread sauce and the cranberry and orange compôte.

'Mm, I adore the smell of onion and bay leaves infusing in milk. It reminds me so much of England.'

'Although Christmas is the time for home and family, don't you sometimes long to escape up into the mountains with friends and celebrate simply with a cosy meal of Raclette and a bottle of Fendant?'

'Maybe because I could, I choose not to. I'm so lucky to have that option. If I decided to duck out of the occasional Christmas, it's a given that my sister or you and Rich would have the Elderly Ps round. It's when you don't have choice that you feel trapped.' I felt her eyes on me as I stirred the fragrant simmering sauce, careful that it didn't catch on the base of the pan.

I thought of her Swiss Alps, interlinked with the Savoy Alps that I knew from university days. I felt an ache of nostalgia that only served to add to my melancholy.

Christmas Day itself was testing. I was on edge not only with the pressure of cooking and serving the lunch, but also because of a great emptiness inside me. I missed Benjamin dreadfully but didn't want to acknowledge it.

The final straw came after the meal when Tricia and the boys cleared away and I led the oldies into the drawing room to the traditional present-opening in front of the roaring fire. The fire smouldered miserably in the hearth. The room felt as cold as charity. Mark had neglected to stoke it with logs before lunch, as requested.

Was I over the top? Probably. I didn't care. I led him by the arm into the snug and closed the door. Yes, I shouldn't have done that. I wanted to slap him.

'How could you?' I hissed. 'All you had to do was put a few fucking logs on the fire.' Did I just use the F word? He shrugged off my hand and stared back at me without expression other than a hardness in his eyes. I felt all the more chilled with shame at my outburst but even more with fear of what lay behind those eyes.

'Don't take your frustration out on us.' Mark spoke softly, which made it all the more menacing. He left the room.

*

In those flat grey days that followed Twelfth Night, after the decorations were carefully packed away, I stood at the kitchen table and gazed out into the resting garden. Tears flowed unchecked.

'Have a good cry,' my father would have said. 'Then do something.'

What? I wandered up to my study and gazed at the skeletal beech tree. I ached. No, my womb ached. I turned to the double bed where last Benjamin and I had lain, lifted the duvet and climbed, fully clothed, into its comfort.

This is the onset of depression. I have to fight it. My arms enfolded my body and then slowly but deliberately my hands slid down over my breasts, over my belly and my right hand sought that aching spot. Afterwards, I lay back but my desire was far from appeased. I longed for Benjamin beside me, inside me, but I needed more than sex, as I'd discovered a few days earlier.

Richard had phoned me from the office.

'I've got the post-Christmas blues, so why don't we dress up and I'll take you out to dinner tonight?' Surprised, I agreed. Moments after ending the call, I regretted it. I just wasn't in the mood, but it was a kind thought, so get on with it, woman, and be grateful.

'Thank you for doing Christmas so brilliantly. Everyone really appreciated it.' He raised his glass towards me. 'So here's to you, my darling, thank you.' I smiled my thanks across the crisp white tablecloth in the post-festive emptiness of our favourite restaurant.

'I enjoy having everyone together,' I shrugged but smiled.

'Yes, but we take you for granted, and tonight I want to say how much I love you.'

Oh, no. I cringed inwardly. *This isn't really you. Don't pretend.* I felt embarrassed as he awkwardly reached over and caressed my hand. I stroked his in return and gently changed the subject to talking about the boys, recently returned to school and uni. *Anything but romance, please.*

I should have anticipated what was to come. The buzz of his electric shaver in the bathroom alerted me that tonight there would be sex for the first time since his heart trouble. I lay on my side reading my book and felt him slide into bed beside me. He put out his bedside lamp, rolled towards my uncompromising back and nuzzled my neck.

'Night-night,' I whispered without turning. 'Thanks for a lovely evening. You're tired, so you get off to sleep and I'll just finish this chapter.' I bounced round and gave him a peck on the cheek then returned to my book. It didn't take a genius to spot a rebuff like that, and with a stroke of my hair, Richard sighed, turned over and within a few minutes his gentle snoring began.

For days afterwards, I hovered over my mobile. Just send a simple text. That's all it needed. It must be the same for people who have given up drugs, cigarettes, alcohol. Just when they think they've mastered their addiction, that's when the longing becomes hardest to resist.

The call from Jeremy broke into my self-absorption. Back at uni, he sounded really revved up, fizzing with life. I envied him. Next, the knife thrust, though he was oblivious to the impact of his news.

'Great stuff, Benny's got a few days off this week so I've asked him down for a couple of concerts. He can hang out at my place.' The jealousy gnawed. I hated Jeremy calling him Benny. Why would Benjamin stay at our flat?

After the call I unpicked my emotions. Why should it matter that my ex-lover should enjoy a few days of music staying with my son? But it did. Mattered a lot. Mattered a hell of a lot. That was it. The catalyst. I reached for my mobile.

In urgent need of tuition. Free Wed, Thurs, Fri. Let me know. G Yes, the days when he was due to go to Birmingham. *Send.*

No reply for the next few hours. I turned to my piano and shocked myself at how rusty my playing had become. I persisted for an hour then in disgust wandered into my kitchen, leant against the Aga and calculated what ingredients I had in store for a baking session. Soothing baking.

The comforting aroma of marmalade cake suffused the kitchen when my mobile trilled once in my pocket. I made myself a tea in case it was the wrong answer. I sat at the table, the steaming mug before me. I opened the message.

OK Wed. Usual time?

How bald is a text message. No intimation of emotion. Was it a reluctant 'OK', an enthusiastic 'OK', or just a resigned 'OK'?

*

The horns speak sadly, first admonishing then regretful, countered by the lighter pizzicato of strings. The peace is soon dispelled as the full orchestra piles in like dogs after a fleeing hind and pulls up triumphantly at the kill.

Georgina is distracted by Richard as he loosens the patterned yellow tie that she bought in Burlington Arcade for his Christmas stocking. He fiddles with the top button of his shirt. His look of desperation disturbs her. She wants to grasp his phone, to read the message. If he refuses, she will know it is about her. But it is too late and her spirits plunge as she anticipates the coming *Adagietto*.

Her malevolent gaze beams across the auditorium to Benjamin.

Chapter Thirteen – Benjamin's Story

Between the movements, the conductor wipes his face with a white handkerchief and pauses until the coughing stops. Benjamin, bow resting on his knees, waits for the horns to begin before he and the other string sections enter, delicately plucking the notes of the *Scherzo* as it unfolds into a witty celebration. Imagined or no, he feels Georgie's eyes upon him. His mood is spikey and, in sympathy, the music tumbles into discord.

*

Discordant. That described me at the beginning of the season when Jeremy's text landed. I was in a bad place, snapping at fellow players, avoiding the pub after concerts. I was totally pissed off with Georgie for the way she'd ended things. Furious that I just couldn't get her out of my head. The physical ache for her astonished me but I missed more than the sex. Once I even phoned their house when I guessed nobody was home, just to hear her voice on the answering machine. What sort of a wuss does that? It nearly backfired. Unexpectedly, Mark was home and picked up. I killed the call. Would he have recognised my number if he dialled 1471?

The hardest thing was seeing her at concerts. Always with Richard. Some meetings couldn't be avoided.

'Hi, Benjamin, how're you doing?' called out Richard at the pre-concert reception to celebrate the opening of the new season in September. His sharp features were even more drawn since he had lost weight, but otherwise he seemed not too bad after his illness. Georgie held back and, as I walked towards them in response to Richard's greeting, she turned and moved swiftly with hand outstretched to the orchestra manager in an adjacent group.

'Richard. More importantly, how are you doing?'

'Oh, not too badly, thanks. I'm lucky it was just a warning. Frightened the hell out of me though. Georgina too, though she now uses it as a weapon to make sure I eat and drink less, get more exercise and don't work silly hours at the office,' he grinned, looked over his shoulder to Georgie, noted her disappearance. He shrugged and rolled his eyes: *Women, eh*?

'Well, we're all delighted to see you so recovered,' was my not totally genuine reply. I sought something further to add, something that didn't relate to Georgie who was foremost in my thoughts. He got there first.

'So, Benjamin, when are you getting back to coaching Jeremy and Georgina again?' The question I dreaded. 'By the way, sorry to hear about the loss of your Gran.'

'Well ...' Christ, why hadn't I prepared for this? 'Jeremy is back at uni any time now and unfortunately our rehearsal schedule is pretty manic at present, with the new season and the tour coming up. Sadly, it doesn't seem like I'll have much chance to get over to coach Georgina just now.' I presented him with what I hoped was a rueful smile.

'That's a pity. Georgina could do with something to brighten her up. Nursing me seems to have dragged her down and she blossomed back in the summer when she got back into her piano playing.' The reminder of that blossoming increased my resentment. Luckily, the steward announced the ten minute bell had sounded. I excused myself and with relief headed back-stage.

So, she was feeling down, was she? Good. I felt a frisson of pleasure that I wasn't the only one totally fucked up. Did she miss me? Was ending it really all about Richard's illness? Did she have second thoughts about a lover on the side? Perhaps she was simply bored with the affair? Was it all about that last time together?

*

Why did I accept Jeremy's invitation to travel down to Birmingham in October? True, an opportunity to see Simon Rattle was not to be missed. In reality I wanted to discover what Georgie was up to.

Mum and Dad were thrilled that I'd be staying with them overnight, albeit arriving late and leaving early. Nonetheless, it was a relief to have only an hour or so with them before bed; it would restrict the probing questions Mum just can't resist. She longs for me to 'find someone' and be settled.

It was a year or so since I'd been in the centre of Birmingham and I always feel nostalgic as I walk from the station past the classical Victorian Town Hall, now soot-free but no longer home to the big symphony concerts. It was a cold evening as I pressed on towards the massive complex that houses Symphony Hall. Like a swaggering cruise ship entering the waterways of Venice, it looms large over the main flow of Broad Street and even more so over the prettified, once industrial canal that lies behind it.

I walked down the tow-path to the traditional pub preferred by students and older musicians alike and there met Jeremy surrounded by his mates. He introduced me and I observed his buzz from presenting me as a Second Violin in one of the country's top bands. Whatever. I ordered a half of something cold and the recommended lasagne and chips.

'Cool you could be here, Benny,' he grinned with face alight. As he babbled on endlessly, I looked into his eyes, feigning interest, and was intrigued to notice how closely they resembled his mother's. He continued without cease and I looked more closely at his features, at his hair, hanging untidily over the collar of his jacket. Ruffled, like Georgie's after sex. I realised he'd asked me a question.

'Sorry, it's a bit loud in here. Say again?'

'Mum and Dad. Have you seen them?'

'Sure, they were at the sponsors' bash at the start of the season. Didn't have long with them though. Your Dad looked better than I'd expected.' Please change the subject. But no.

'Right on. He's been bloody lucky to get away with it. That's what we all think. Maybe he'll go easy on the job now he's been warned. Too late for me or Mark though,' he added somewhat wistfully. 'It would have been great to have had Dad around when we were growing up but there was always something that kept him away from home.' I wondered fleetingly if Richard's 'away from home' had included another woman at some point, then dismissed it without knowing why. Does the adulterer have 'adulterer' tattooed on his forehead? I don't think so.

The concert was full of Rattle supporters from his earlier stint with Birmingham's orchestra and the audience went wild with applause. Everyone was on a high after such an amazing performance and Jeremy was equally carried away, shouting above the noise, slinging an arm around my shoulder with sheer exuberance. That closeness to the boy, to Georgie's boy, stimulated warm feelings that I didn't reckon on. Impulsively I covered his hand with mine. It was soft to touch. Slightly uneasy at my reaction, I muttered something and we separated and moved on as the audience surged out.

It was mayhem as we followed the crowd out into the now bitterly cold night. We were surrounded by loads of people, some couples, some in straggling groups wearing uniform t-shirts and bizarre head-dresses, unmistakeably on a stag or a hen night. What is it with girls that they can walk the streets late at night, totally trashed and half-dressed without expecting trouble?

My bus-stop fell before his and he insisted on waiting with me. Shifting our feet as the night air chilled, we continued our 'informed' analysis of the concert. It was the last thing I needed. Picking over the bones of a performance is pretentious at best but I let it roll, chipping in as Jeremy enthused on. Then, almost as a throw-away, he suggested I should come down again for a concert but next time maybe a different arrangement.

'If you want,' he hesitated, 'you could crash down at mine so that it's easier to get the train back north the next day.' Something flared inside me, something intangible from the past, and I stared at this guy, so much still a boy, with eyes fired with enthusiasm; enthusiasm I'd seen so often with his mother as I pulled her against me. He seemed embarrassed by my gaze and I relaxed away from him.

'Why not, why not? I'd really like that.' With a swift farewell I stepped onto my bus and for the next thirty minutes gazed out at the lit streets of Midlands sprawl wondering where all this was taking me. And I didn't mean the bus.

*

What made me accept that second invitation a month later? It wasn't really the Beethoven Nine that attracted me, though Birmingham has one of the best choruses and without doubt they'd give the *Ode to Joy* loads of wellie. The thought of seeing Jeremy again strangely appealed to me as I trundled on with rehearsals, concerts, the odd tutoring session.

In the meantime there had been no occasion to meet up again with Georgie and Richard. During performances I forced myself not to look up at their seats. But I was conscious of her disturbing presence each time I walked onto the platform. Fucking crazy. A married woman nearly twenty years older than me and, let's face it, no longer in her prime. What's more, a woman who'd wanted out. I'd got to be mad.

I called Jeremy and accepted his invitation.

This time I arrived early afternoon and caught the bus out to student land in the university sector of the city. The flat that Jeremy's parents had found for him was on the ground floor of a double-fronted Edwardian house. None of the bed-sit in a Victorian back-to-back that I'd suffered in my student days. Despite his stuff layered all over the bedroom and sitting room, I easily spotted Georgie's touch in the décor. Even the mugs we drank our tea from were the same as those in the kitchen at Greystones.

'Drop your bag in the bedroom and I'll get us a coffee. It's instant. I can't afford ground,' he excused, pointing at the cafetière, twin to Georgie's, 'but Mum doesn't realise that.'

The bedroom had been decorated in a masculine style and I felt the presence of Georgie in the room's furnishings, particularly the navy and emerald throw that Jeremy had carelessly pulled up over the rumpled double bed. It was the same fabric she had on the bed in her study. Our bed. The image of making love to her aroused me. I dropped my bag on the floor and returned to the sitting room, eyeing the two-seater sofa. I hoped it would pull out into a bed otherwise I'd have a cramped night to come.

'Great place you have here, Jeremy.' I wandered around the white painted room, bright with its large bay window looking onto the front garden, now paved for parking. Large framed prints of paintings by Kandinsky and Klee added vibrancy and Georgie (who else?) had picked out strong primary colours for the sofa, curtains and huge rug which covered much of the wooden flooring. This must have cost a bomb. 'Your landlord has great taste.'

Jeremy laughed.

'My grandparents bought the flat as an investment. It was pretty grim when they found it so Mum got stuck in and this is the result. I'm lucky,' he acknowledged. 'Nearly all my mates have to share and nobody has anything this good. It's great because I can practise here without bothering too many people. The woman upstairs is at work during the day and out most evenings.'

Later I freshened up in his bathroom, simply but well appointed, and definitely in need of my Nan's cleaning skills. We caught the bus into the centre to eat pre-concert in a nearby Italian. As we forked our way through a seafood risotto, I let Jeremy lead the conversation which blathered on about his university life: the lecturers, the modules, fellow students and exams. I chipped in when my opinion was sought, otherwise I let it flow over me, enjoying the food and eyeing others in the restaurant. Early on I spotted a couple of players eating before their performance. I recognised one violinist from my own student days and the other was a well-known trombonist on the music circuit. I wasn't in the mood to talk, so averted my face.

The auditorium was packed for this popular symphony. Familiarity with a favourite piece is double-edged. Your anticipation is all the greater, simply because you know the music and welcome each movement with its change of pace and theme. Therein lies the danger of taking an old friend for granted. For any listener, be they player or music lover, the experience is refined as each conductor brings his own interpretation. Sometimes it disappoints because you prefer what is familiar. I like to be surprised.

That evening I was transfixed as the energetic young conductor drew the most sensitive and inspiring interpretation of Beethoven's Ninth that I've ever heard. The chorus sat in disciplined silence throughout the first three movements then in the famous *Ode to Joy* took the place by storm with its cry, '*Freude!*'.

Was I particularly receptive that night? Did I simply seek an outlet for my messed up emotions? How much did the music contribute to what followed? I can't say, but that is what music does. It stimulates emotion. High, low, joyous, contented, sad. That night I was stirred by Beethoven and on a high.

Uncharacteristically, Jeremy didn't chatter on as we took the bus back to his flat. Both of us knew that each had been moved and in a good way. As he switched on the lamps around the sitting room, he turned to me, almost shyly.

'Look Benny, I'm too fizzing for sleep yet. You've got an early start tomorrow, but before I make up the sofa bed, how about some of the wine you brought?'

Feeling totally relaxed, I ignored the cringe-making 'Benny' and dropped into the sofa with a nod. Before opening the bottle of red, Jeremy put on some music, not so loud to disturb the neighbours, just enough to keep the mood alive.

His choice of music: Richard Strauss's *Vier Letzte Lieder* with the cream-caramel voice of Jesse Norman. The first song, *Frühling*, streamed over us, Norman's ethereal tones luring us on. The purity stirred me as never before. Before I knew it, the soft lighting, the warmth of the wine, the haunting music, all conspired to raise me to a point of acute desire for Georgie.

Jeremy joined me. My free arm lay draped across the back of the sofa. He covered my hand with his. I was surprised, maybe even shocked by this unambiguous move, but didn't recoil. He moved to rest against me. I didn't react but relaxed with the warmth of his body.

We listened to the glorious Strauss. By the violin solo of the third song, with its aching longing, all I saw looking up at me were Georgie's eyes, eyes full of uncertainty, Georgie's hair, hair to be caressed, Georgie's lips, lips parted and full. But this was her son and I held back. Jeremy raised his face to mine. I held my breath. He reached up and stroked my temple. I sighed with resignation. After this, there would be no going back. He reached up and kissed me tentatively and, as I hesitated, those eyes pleaded.

I didn't want this. I never intended this. Was it the frustration of the past months? Was it revenge on his mother? I responded, none too gently, and kissed him long and hard on the mouth. There was no resistance. I wanted the fourth song, *Im Abendrot*, to last forever.

Waking the next morning, I heard the shallow breathing of Jeremy beside me. It had been his first time. I recognised that at once in remembering my initiation by Henry after that Mahler concert so long ago. I turned to see his hair tumbled onto the soft nape of his neck, the duvet half covering white shoulders. God, how like Georgie he looked. I stifled the urge to stroke the hair, to stir him as I felt myself again stirred, but instead slipped out of the large bed and into the bathroom.

'Shall I make you coffee before you go?' he asked with a hesitant smile, sitting up in bed as I returned naked to the bedroom to dress.

'Thanks, but no. I'll grab something at New Street station,' I replied, matter of fact, totally unsure what to say next. What do you say to someone you slept with because he reminds you of his mother? 'Look, last night …'

'Benny, don't say anything,' he blurted out. 'It probably wasn't what you intended. It happened, and I'm glad it did. I wanted it too. I just had no idea you …' He looked acutely embarrassed and I picked up my bag ready to leave.

'Um, look, I'll be in touch,' I smiled unconvincingly. 'Take care. See you later.' Christ, I hate that phrase. Why did I say that?

'See you later,' came the unbelieving response.

*

I sat hunched against the rain-spattered window as the train hurtled north through the flat agricultural landscape of the north Midlands. How did I feel about sex with a virgin gay? Georgie's son. Although he made the first move, did I feel guilty? No, not guilty, just pissed off that in one evening I had further complicated my life.

I hadn't realised he was gay and wondered if she knew. She'd never hinted at it, but she wouldn't have, would she? How would she react? Richard would be horrified to have a shirt-lifter in the family. But Georgie ... she would be devastated to discover that her ex-lover swings both ways and had just deflowered her first-born. This had to be kept under the radar.

It had been some years since my last gay encounter. Always encounters, never affairs. Always purely physical attraction. I never felt emotionally involved, not even with Henry. Emotional involvement wasn't something I wanted or needed, not even with girls. Good sex is good sex. It's exhilarating. Makes you feel great about yourself. And if it isn't good sex, then move on. Not difficult. Not for me. Not then. That was before Georgie.

So, no feeling of guilt. Jeremy was well up for it. It was a rite of passage and if it hadn't been me, it would have been someone else. Though maybe it wasn't totally helpful to my future career that it was me.

What I didn't anticipate was Jeremy falling in love. What a joke.

*

The witty *Scherzo* ends on a sour note. The mournful horns plaintively defend some past misdemeanour until their excuses fade away in embarrassment. The violins hiss into action, leading the attack, and the conductor drives the full force of the orchestra into screaming condemnation before lashing out with a triumphant flourish. The players slump back into their chairs to gather strength, both physical and emotional, for the heart-rending *Adagietto* to come. Benjamin psyches himself up for this movement, which he listens to over again whenever at his lowest ebb. He senses Georgie's hatred streaming down on him and now no longer cares.

Chapter Fourteen – Jeremy's Story

The conductor brings the orchestra to attention. He points his baton to the four French horn players who open the movement with measured optimism while the first violins sit poised to enter with their light-hearted dance. Jeremy watches Benny's decisive fingering as the second violinists pluck *pizzicato* in support.

*

From the moment he accepted my invitation to sleep over after the Beethoven Nine concert, I felt sick with excitement. Bizarrely, as some sort of coping mechanism, I even attempted to clean the flat, the first time since Mum brought her 'treasure' down to blitz the place ahead of the autumn term. Clean towels, clean sheets. I planned to take my duvet and crash out on the sofa-bed.

What did I expect that day? To be honest, probably nothing. Why would I? After all, he was as hetero as they come and I'd seen how the girls in the band eyed him. Yet, there seemed to be nobody in his life (wrong!) and when I was with him I buzzed, I buzzed. A bit like with Grainger, but more fizz. No, that's crap; not at all like with Grainger. Different and much more.

With mugs of coffee in hand we walked around my small flat and I could see that he was impressed by the look of the place. Yesss!

'I'm really lucky.' God, I sounded like an apologetic spoilt kid. 'When Mima told me that she and Poppa were investing in this flat, she insisted that it was on condition that Mum did the place up. I think she feared that I'd make such a cock of it that they'd never get their money back when they came to sell it.'

'Yes, I can see your mother's touch everywhere. She has a good eye,' he spoke softly, as he stroked his hand over the tweed of the armchair.

While he freshened up, I sorted away our coffee mugs, trying to give him space. Without his shirt, his smooth wiry body looked really fit and I tried not to stare at him as he wandered between the bedroom and bathroom. To my discomfort I realised my feelings for him had become physically apparent.

Before the concert, we ate at an Italian. I was so nervous that I rabbited on about everything and nothing: essays, lecturers, stuff. He seemed interested. Really? I wonder.

The music world was afire with enthusiasm for the concert's young conductor. Benny knew of his reputation but hadn't seen this rising star perform. No doubt about it, the guy was a knock-out and held the audience in his hand. They went wild as he took his bow. The orchestra, soloists and chorus well deserved the standing ovation – well, let's say a few rows of people were on their feet applauding, this is buttoned-up Britain after all.

The euphoria continued as we left the hall and sat side by side in silence on the homeward bus. No words could describe my elation. The music, the performance and now Benny beside me heading back to my place. My body tingled. With fear, with anticipation? I'm not sure I know the difference at moments like that. Yes, I felt sick, but in a good way.

I'd given way to extravagance and left the heating on all evening. As we entered the flat, warmth welcomed and I relaxed. It was just after eleven but no way was I ready for sleep. As I switched on the lamps, I thanked Mum for choosing colours, lighting, just right for that evening's mood. I don't suppose, though, that she had seduction in mind when she pulled her scheme together.

What's the best music at a time like that? I steered away from modern stuff, but was uncertain what to choose. My thumb shuttled through albums, I slipped my iPod into its dock and pressed 'Play'. What made me choose Strauss's *Four Last Songs*? Not a clue.

It was all so, so easy. I handed him a glass of the wine he'd brought me and debated whether to sit opposite or next to him on the sofa. He sat, one arm resting along the back of the sofa. I chose to join him.

'Ah, *Vier Letzte Lieder...*' he spoke the German almost as a sigh, then stopped. Had he intended to say more?

'It does things for me,' I said softly, not wishing to disturb the moment. I gazed into his eyes, seeking understanding of my inept explanation. He smiled in acknowledgement. His arm curved loosely around my shoulder and I moved my hand to cover his. My heart thudded at such boldness and staring at him I tensed myself for a rebuff. None came. I felt my temples pulse as I deliberately relaxed against him. I expected him to extricate himself. He didn't.

We lay close, listening to that glorious voice, until the third song when I dared to gaze into his dark-brown eyes and for a long moment they searched mine with puzzlement. This was the moment and my instinct drove me on. I reached my face up to his. He didn't withdraw. Emboldened, I stroked his temple. He sighed briefly. I pressed my body against his as I kissed him full on the mouth feeling his face rasp against mine. What was I doing? Was I mad? Finally Benny responded, with rough enthusiasm.

That first time together, I was almost out of my head. I was emotionally and physically exhausted and lay awake for hours, conscious of Benny's steady breathing, his body moving against me as he stirred during the night. I felt terrified. My first time. Was I any good? Did I do it right? Was this a dreadful embarrassing mistake?

The next morning he showered before I woke and then refused my offer of breakfast. Seeing him standing naked in my bedroom generated a weird mixture of shyness and longing. Then came the doubt. Did he regret it? He started to mumble something and I interrupted him.

'Look Benny, what went on last night. I've never ... Let's just forget it happened, if you want ...' I had to give him an out. Perhaps it had all been a dreadful mistake. Who knew that he was gay?

'Well, um, you're probably right. It'll be OK. I'll be in touch to meet up for a concert soon.' His voice lapsed into an embarrassed silence and he gripped my shoulder in farewell. 'See you later.'

'Yes, great, that'd be good. See you later,' I responded unconvincingly. What in fuck's name had we done? Where did we go from here?

*

Going home for Christmas was always going to be hard. It was a short holiday, with loads of people to see, things to do and little opportunity to see Benjamin. The few weeks since the Beethoven concert, since we came together, had been agonising. I started by sending him a text. His response was low key but not unkind. I gathered courage to phone him but it always went to voice-mail. Was that discretion or second thoughts?

During the holiday, there wouldn't be time for our trio sessions and in any case Mum would want to keep the drawing room clear for her tree. It's a large room with two massive sofas as well as the baby grand, and we always use it at Christmas, even though it's one of the coldest rooms in the house. Here is where the family settles after Christmas lunch, totally stuffed, and opens presents in front of a blazing fire. Well it would have been blazing had Mark, designated fire monitor, remembered to stoke it as we went into the dining room to eat. Instead, we trooped in to find barely salvageable embers smouldering behind the fireguard and a decided nip in the air. It was nothing to the frost emanating from Mum. She and Mark withdrew into the snug to exchange heated words.

Being British, the rest of the family carried on regardless. Soon the re-kindled fire, together with the warmth of our bodies stoked by copious rich food and drink, restored a glow into the proceedings. Except for Mark.

Not wishing to draw attention to his absence as we all exchanged gifts, I pulled his glittering pile to one side and, as attention was focused elsewhere, probably Aunt Tricia holding forth, I slipped out with his presents and discovered him up in his room, engrossed in his laptop.

Ungraciously, he nodded as I laid the parcels on his bed.

'What is it with you?' I stood with my hand on the open door, about to return to the family. He responded with a shrug and a contemptuous grimace.

'No, seriously. Can't you make a fucking effort for once?' I walked back into his room and re-closed the door in anticipation of imminent raised voices. I'd had enough of him and, Christmas Day or no Christmas Day, he was going to hear it from me.

'Since you got back from school you've behaved like a nob. Hardly a civil word to any of us and the way you treat Mum … Just think how much work she puts into Christmas for all the family.'

He rose swiftly and walked at me. He stood close. He's caught me up in height. I could smell the wine on his breath as he stared hard into my eyes, his face taut with anger.

'You haven't a fucking clue, have you? What planet are you on? You're all the same, the whole bloody family, so totally seduced by your music that none of you can see what's under your nose. And she of all people, playing happy families. You're just too thick to see through her – or don't want to.'

I stood stock still, shaken by his outburst. Where had that come from? I opened my mouth to ask what the hell he was talking about, when Dad opened the door.

'What's going on guys? Christmas Day is no time for squabbles. Come on Mark, get downstairs and open your presents and thank people properly. Where are your manners, lad?' In his irritation, he lapsed into his northern accent, sounding just like Grandad.

Mark paused, gave me a final withering stare, switched on a smile for Dad, cuffing his arm in a sign of apology, and gathered up his presents.

I walked out of his room, down the chilly staircase and back into the warmth of the family chatter, my head reeling with questions. What didn't I know?

Now of course, I do know. How did he find out? And when?

Must have been before Christmas but I can't believe they were at it in November when Benny and I got together. How can you make love with two different people at the same time? Two *really* different people. Are bi-sexuals really that promiscuous? There was nothing casual about me and Benny. He cared for me. I'm sure he did. There, already I'm using the past tense.

*

Jeremy is dragged back to the present by a momentary lull in the music. The horns' entreaty for calm is countered by the orchestra's harrying face-off before the players all come together, ending the movement with a flourish.

The girl distracts him once more as she reaches down to lift her bag onto her knee and surreptitiously opens it to view her glowing phone. *For God's sake, switch it off*, he pleads in his head. How dare she desecrate the coming *Adagietto,* the most beautiful part of the whole symphony.

Chapter Fifteen – The Girl's Story

The audience shuffles and coughs; the musicians surreptitiously stretch aching muscles in hands, arms, shoulders, mouths. With deep satisfaction, the girl observes the man's reaction to the message. She watches him fiddle with his tie, a sign of unease.

May it choke you, the girl invokes.

The orchestra sets off again, the string players plucking their strings, the heads of the woodwind players bobbing chirpily, echoing her inner excitement. Tonight she would see her revenge played out publicly and to maximum effect. She brightens up.

This is going to be mega.

*

How ironic. After graduation even I struggled to get a job in my chosen subject. Despite Mum's marketing and sales contacts, it was always the same: they wanted someone with experience. I was always up against the Samanthas whose father's 'contacts' ensured placements with big brand pharma or FMCG companies. But in any case, I couldn't afford an unpaid internship. Not an option. That's why all my holiday jobs brought in money but no way helped my CV.

In the end, The Bear went over Mum's head and suggested to me that I could join his company as a marketing junior. I hesitated. His was a small company and I guessed that his idea of marketing would hardly match up with what today's business world needed. And really, traffic management is hardly sexy. I'd thoughts of working in something meatier. Maybe in one of the big banks. Somewhere to make serious money.

'It'll give you a starting point,' he said. 'After a year you can move on with some experience under your belt. That's if you'd want to.'

I promised to think about it. In reality, I needed to discuss it with Mum.

'What do you know about his set-up?' We sat out on the slabs Mum grandly calls her patio. 'I don't want to end up doing all the crap jobs.'

Mum tapped ash from her cigarette, sipped at her Gold Blend and sighed. She'd been furious when The Bear told her of his offer. She resented owing him anything, but she was a realist.

'Doing crap is part of everyone's first job. Get over it.' I rolled my eyes in resignation. 'It's bloody good of him to offer you this. You are aware he's creating a job that doesn't exist?' Exactly what I feared.

That first day was pretty difficult. Everyone knew that I'd walked into a new position. I quickly discovered that some people resented the fact, especially when there was a block on recruitment even if someone left. In consequence, some parts of the business were overloaded with work.

The worst were the women, especially the older women who were convinced I was the boss's new bit of stuff. I suppose those who'd worked there for years and had known his late wife, Sonia, might suspect that. Being on the wrong side of opinion was nothing new to me so I just got on with my work and ignored them. This was not the place to be snapping little fingers.

For some weird reason, Mum insisted that I used my second name, Sarah.

'Why?'

'Sarah has a more authoritative ring,' was her lame reply.

'That's a load of crap.'

What was the real reason? She continued to be evasive and, to my astonishment, The Bear agreed with her, muttering something about 'past history'. So in the office I was called Sarah.

In the event, it was better than I'd expected. Sure, his main idea of marketing the company was schmoozing potential customers with meals and corporate entertaining of the sporting kind, but there was room for other stuff too. Their on-line presence was pathetic so I knew I really could make a difference there.

He recognised that, if I was to be of any use, they had to train me up. I spent time shadowing various members of the team and quickly got my head around the basics. I sat with him and discussed the fundamentals picked up at uni and, with surprising patience, he worked through what might suit his business and what was inappropriate. This won me brownie points and, more importantly, a recognition that I could contribute.

My desk was in the middle of the open-plan office where everyone sat, except The Bear, his PA, and the finance director. If he wanted to discuss something he would come to his door and shout at who-ever. When it was my turn, I would feel the eyes of the office as I picked up my pad and diary and walked between the desks into his office.

Fuck them, I'd say to myself, my face betraying no emotion as I closed the door behind me.

I found my niche with the drive for new business. I'm good at putting together presentations for potential clients, looking after the IT and showing examples of past work. He and I work well together and I've developed an energetic delivery. It attracts the male prospects but I make sure it doesn't piss off the increasing number of female decision makers.

We ended up travelling together quite a lot and I enjoyed the long drives in the car. We were private and could talk about things other than work. I told him stuff I'd never discussed with Mum. Sitting at his side, observing his profile as he watched the road ahead, I also learnt more about him.

It was when I probed about my father that his face hardened.

'Did you ever meet my Dad?' After a slight pause he grunted his assent.

'Did you get to know him?' I pushed on, despite suspecting that he didn't want to talk about this and probably wouldn't reveal much.

'Look, you don't want to go there. Just leave things be. He's still paying you an allowance. Just drop it.'

I sat in silence as his Jag devoured more motorway miles, but I couldn't drop it.

'You must have known him, otherwise why would you have pushed Mum to extort so much money out of him over the years. I reckon you do know him and you've something against him.'

From the tightening of his hands on the steering wheel and the frown, I saw I'd hit home.

'Extort! Extort! That's an ugly word. Your Mum doesn't see it as extortion and nor do I. You're entitled to his financial support. For God's sake, he's given you no other support over the years.' I remained silent, wanting him to expand further.

'How I feel doesn't matter. It was your Mum and you that were my only concern.' I reflected for another mile or so and concluded he was lying. I needed to discover more about his relationship with my father, both years ago and now. But that would be a step too far. Enough for now.

*

I was dead pleased with our recent big win in London. From the outset I worked alongside the boss and for the first time created a pitch campaign which amused him and irritated the shit out of some of his colleagues, who'd always managed in the past without one, thank you very much. Tim, one of the younger guys, was supportive and countered the scarcely concealed criticism.

'Why don't we give it a go? There's time and this is one of the biggest projects that's out there at the moment. You lot can continue to work things through in your own way and we can just dovetail this into what you come up with. Best of both worlds?' What a diplomat. I'd have told them to get into fucking line.

My input was to initiate the research, which went far deeper than usual. Tim worked with me and together we travelled to the location and drilled down into the sensitivities of the place and the people. Road improvement done badly not only cocks up the traffic but also stirs up a load of shit with the locals. I wanted us to demonstrate not only the best traffic solution but also how we got there. That would give our business the point of difference to screw our competitors.

'This all sounds a bit touchy-feely to me,' was the verdict when Tim and I presented our findings and recommendations. I had to curb my impatience and remind myself I was in Sarah mode, not at home firing off over the kitchen table.

'Maybe it does to you,' my voice measured and not dismissive, 'but people who are going to recommend our bid also have to consider the costly PR campaign they'll need to fund if this project goes tits up.'

'Sarah's right.' Tim quickly moved to underpin my argument. 'We guess the solution we present won't be greatly different from any other consultancy so we have to prove that where there is a difference, it's based on detailed research and understanding of their locality.' We waited while our paper was studied. I broke the silence.

'If we don't win this pitch, in a couple of months' time we're going to be struggling to find work for the team when the current jobs are completed. It would be a pity to lose talent.' I alluded to the potential threat of job losses which have been part of life for the last six years.

So we won the day and, eventually, the project. However, once the euphoria had settled, The Bear was off again, his sights firmly fixed on the future. A couple of weeks later, as we wrapped up the de-brief on the pitch process and the room emptied, he turned to me with a mysterious smile.

'Pack your bag for a couple of nights. I want to show you some new opportunities.'

Two days later, we headed north, first meandering around the confusion of the Midlands with miles of industry sprawling either side of the M6.

That night was spent in Birmingham with dinner in a penthouse restaurant offering an extensive but frankly uninspiring view of lit streets and dark rooftops spreading to the unseen horizon. He talked about the company and revealed his ambition.

'We've got to grow this business. London is the logical option to give us a national platform, but it would cost too much to set up there. Despite the recent win in East London, we're seen as a provincial set-up. Unfortunately there isn't enough new work about for us to expand just within the South. We've got to look beyond. That means acquisition.'

It explained the address plumbed into his satnav which earlier that day took us into the Victorian squares of Birmingham's Jewellery Quarter. He weaved in and around the narrow streets and at one point responded to *You have reached your destination* by stopping, double parked. He gazed up at a converted warehouse with a discreet but arty nameplate beside a stylish entrance. I waited in vain for an explanation but was not prepared to ask for one.

The next morning we headed further north, back to his home patch. Here he trawled the area without need for his satnav and we whizzed between former mill towns and explored city centres, apparently with some hidden agenda, still not revealed. Again, we lurked outside an office building, this time on the edge of one of the large industrial towns, once big in the wool trade, or was it cotton?

All very interesting, but I was frustrated. Why take me with him? What wasn't he sharing?

The office knew we'd both been away, but not where or why. And he didn't want them to know. I was quietly amused by the speculation and played it deadpan. Before long, he had me working on a confidential project, so confidential that I was moved into his PA's office. She was pissed off that I'd invaded her private domain, but tough. It served to fuel further gossip about the boss's tart.

He had identified a northern outfit with a good reputation but struggling, according to the grapevine. It was located in his home town and he'd worked there at the beginning of his career. Was it the office we'd parked outside?

It was my job to research as much as possible about the company: its clients, team, strengths and of course, its weaknesses. It was great. I loved the research process but, above all, I relished the secrecy.

*

Suddenly the music is over, however as nobody claps, she deflates, realising that it isn't the end yet.

How much longer, for God's sake?

During the short pause, she itches to check the time on her phone but hesitates. A single vibration in her bag against her feet. A message. Decisively she bends down and raises the capacious leaf-green bag onto her lap. Gently she unclips the clasp. With the phone safely nestled inside, she peers down and the sender's name blazes up at her. She smiles.

Swiftly she opens and reads the message, indifferent to the fact that the glow will be noticeable at least to Mr Grumpy at her side. The bag is re-closed and returned to the floor. She leans back, her smile of satisfaction probably not visible to the sender, seated high up in the audience before her.

FOURTH MOVEMENT *Adagietto*

Chapter Sixteen – Richard's Story

The hall holds its breath. The conductor pauses to contrast the masterly close of the previous *Scherzo* and heighten anticipation for Mahler's intense *Adagietto* and the pain to come.

The tenderness of the opening harp and strings evokes utter despair in Richard. He stalls his response to Mulligan's warning. During this quiet passage, it would be impossible to tap in a reply without being spotted and reviled by the audience, let alone Georgina.

The music evolves into anguished yearning and Richard cannot purge the image of Aschenbach, seated in pathetic isolation among the *fin de siècle* elegance of the Venice Lido, his life ebbing away along with his hopes.

*

Oh God, please find me a way out of this. It mustn't end like this, in total failure. How do I tell the family? Georgina questioning why I need to hand the business over to Mulligan; Jeremy, bewilderment that all that was solid is evaporating; scorn, yes, deep scorn, that's all I expect from Mark.

Mum will listen, not understand and worry about what's to become of us, and of course, what people in the town will say. Always one for what others might think. Dad will shut it out. He doesn't understand business today, he claims. In reality, he doesn't want to know. And why should he? He's old and had his share of worries over the years. This is for me to sort.

It's all happening too quickly. I need a bit longer. We'll make the pitch list for other projects. None will be massive, even if we win them, but at least it would keep things going for a while. Maybe Mulligan is right. Perhaps our size of business is too small for today's world. Double dip, treble dip, the whole economy is shot to hell. This is not how it was meant to be.

How will the team react? Apart from Tom and Jason, the rest haven't a clue what we're up against. Are those two fully on-side? I'm not totally convinced. Can't blame them with family and mortgage around their necks. In this climate they've got to follow the money. Mulligan will retain the majority of staff but the higher salaried people are at greater risk unless they can bring something extra to the party.

Tom has been having time off lately, visiting family he said. Going for interviews? Christ, perhaps even meeting with Mulligan? If he's been giving insider information then I am well and truly shafted. Is that how Mulligan grasped the figures so quickly? And the trip to Amberley. Tom knew that Georgina and I were taking Ian away for the night. Fucking bastard. Is Jason involved too? Trust nobody, that's what Dad always said. Too right.

*

The insidious threat of the music builds, subsides, before strengthening into an insistent undertow. Richard's energy drains away and he slumps deeper into his seat. The pathos of the music seizes him and he looks into Georgina's eyes as she leans towards him, her hand closing over his. She holds his gaze until he shifts his eyes to the players below, too ashamed to accept her deep concern.

*

Georgina doesn't deserve this. I've let her down, again. Only this time she will discover the whole wretched story. After the deal is agreed, due diligence will reveal my payments out of the business to Melanie's lawyers. Could Mulligan still be in touch with her? Can I trust him not to reveal the girl, even if I agree to his terms? It would cut Georgina to the heart to discover that I had a child with another woman, and worse, a daughter. But not hers.

I've never seen grief like Georgina's when they wheeled her into theatre, knowing that our baby was already dead. I felt intense sadness too, though nothing like Georgina's. I can't imagine what a mother must go through after months with a living child inside her, then to realise it's dead.

Years later, I learnt how that stillbirth had affected us so differently. Georgina had gone to bed early after a particularly rowdy evening with the boys. As I slid beneath the duvet, trying not to disturb her, she turned towards me.

'Today would have been Mary's tenth birthday.' She waited for my comment. My heart dropped. There would be no right answer. I felt immediate guilt. The day had never lodged in my conscience. For ten years Georgina had never raised the date, never even spoken of the stillborn child. I read that as a topic off-limits.

'Ten years? I'm sorry, darling, I'd forgotten the date.'

Why would I want to remember the exact date? Anyway, it wasn't the day of her birth, it was a death. A day to forget, surely? I held my tongue.

The darkness lay heavy with hurt and accusation. I remembered the other baby girl, the one born to Melanie, my daughter, Penny. The guilt of not remembering Mary's death resurrected my unease at not acknowledging my first daughter. I reckoned she must be around twelve now. My curiosity roused, I played with the idea of discovering more about Penny. Was she bright, did she take after me or Melanie?

The next morning, as the alarm shuddered the household into action, I reflected further. The pundits on the *Today* programme faded as I weighed up the possibility of meeting my daughter and concluded: *No, not your brightest idea, Richard. Leave well alone.*

Unfortunately, the seed was sown and for days afterwards I tussled with the notion of finding the girl. Not to meet her, no, just to observe her. I had no idea where she lived. I guessed that she and her mother were still in the Southampton area. She'd be at senior school now, a state school. From the internet I gleaned a certain amount of information, but it was pure luck that my trawl revealed press coverage of one particular school's prize day that featured some of the winners, including a photograph of the named winner of the Junior Debating Society's Cup, Melanie's daughter. So, articulate. Well, brought up by Melanie, she's bound to be a lippy kid.

The school's website highlighted forthcoming events. I agonised over travelling down simply to observe, in reality to spy on her. Contact with her would be wrong at so many levels, and no way did I want to meet Melanie.

The school was staging a fund-raiser open to the public, part car-boot sale with a variety show in the afternoon. I could lose myself in the crowd. In the end, I went, unsure whether it would be a total waste of time or a horrendous mistake, were I recognised. I escaped from home that Saturday with the excuse of meeting former Conningsbury colleagues for a lunch-time reunion down south. The school playing fields were already packed when I arrived half an hour before the show. With plastic beaker of cola to hold against my face should I suddenly come up against Melanie, I wandered around the field. My focus was not on the sale tables but on the faces of the women. If I could spot Melanie first, I would find her daughter, my daughter.

They stood in a group of parents with school kids dressed in their maroon and sky blue uniforms. Melanie was side-on to me. She had kept her looks during the intervening years. So which was her daughter? One girl stood slightly apart. Bored, she turned back to the group and touched Melanie's arm. Seeing her full on was a shock. Apart from the blond hair, her features strongly resembled those of my sister around that age. So this was my daughter, Penny.

I withdrew further into the crowd to watch at a more circumspect distance. She was slim, medium height and moved confidently. The two headed towards the seating in front of the stage and the girl split away to join the entertainers. I sat on the back row, ready for a quick exit.

The show consisted of performances by the school orchestra, not bad at all, and the choir, very good. It was a mixture of music and songs from the shows and a medley of classical music used in TV commercials. Light and easy. My daughter stood among the choir and then came forward to sing a duet with an older girl. Her voice projected strongly from the first note and she moved gently but not ostentatiously with the rhythm of the music. Pride flared through me and I had to resist the urge to stand and applaud. Instead, I slipped away and drove home to my family.

I played Beethoven on that journey northwards. The glimpse of Penny had generated so many questions, so many possibilities. I let my imagination run. Could I introduce myself into her life at this late stage? Was she curious to meet me? Would she enjoy two brothers in her life? I could help guide her as she moved through school study into higher education into a career. The opportunities flowed and did so until exhausted. Reality struck. The two gatekeepers would be Melanie and Georgina. The first was unlikely to swerve from her resolution to go it alone; the second would be destroyed by the knowledge I had fathered a daughter with another woman just as I married her. She would have no room in her heart to accept the girl into our family.

No, the decision was reached all those years ago. My place was with Georgina and the boys. My daughter was not part of that life.

*

His memory of duty is echoed in the return of the insistent strings, bows dipping rhythmically like oars. The sound lightens to the white hope of salvation. Surreal sensations engulf Richard before the music softly descends once again into profound loss. Such was the close of the most beautiful piece created by Mahler, written not to commemorate sorrow but as a token of love for his wife, Alma. The wife he sought to control. His cheating wife, Alma.

As the conductor transfers without pause into the final movement, Richard's whole body is assailed by a shuddering flash of cold sweat and he lets out an involuntary low moan.

Chapter Seventeen – Georgina's Story

She shrinks back into her seat as the *Adagietto* opens. This is not the moment to retrieve Richard's phone. They sit within the sightline of much of the audience and it would be a sacrilege to intrude on this, the most passionate part of Mahler's Fifth. The music flows over her as the caress of silk chiffon across her skin. It re-awakens her ache. That reluctant ache, deep inside.

*

Benjamin looked strained as I opened the door that January morning. He stood there in the cold, unsmiling, a bright pink scarf wound around his neck, the collar of his navy woollen jacket pulled up around his ears. I stood aside and invited him into the warm kitchen, where I took his outdoor things. As I hung them in the boot room, I resisted the temptation to bury my face in the softness and smell of his scarf.

He leaned his back against the Aga as I prepared coffee and laid out my marmalade cake.

'So, here we are. Again?'

Embarrassed, I nodded agreement.

'What was it Georgie? Why didn't you return my calls, my messages? It wasn't only because of Richard's illness, was it?' The edge to his voice betrayed anger just below the surface.

'I honestly don't know what to say.' I poured boiling water into the cafetière. My response came out as a disconnected jumble. 'Sorry sounds so feeble. I had to do it. Even before Richard had his attack, I felt guilty about what we were doing.'

Benjamin said nothing, just looked into my eyes.

'I'd never been unfaithful before. Richard isn't a bad person. He didn't deserve that.'

Benjamin rolled his eyes and walked to the window. He looked towards the distant moors, his hands gripping his slender hips.

'Benjamin, just listen. I find it really difficult to explain. I'm afraid it's all coming out wrong. You awoke new emotions, something that Richard has never been able to give me. It's not his fault; he just isn't made like that. Then our last day together, before the boys' summer holidays, something happened to make me stop and think again about what I stood to lose, that it was all wrong.' I continued fussing with the coffee ritual and pressed down the plunger for emphasis.

He twisted round as if to speak, hesitated and returned to the warmth of the Aga. He spoke with a voice harsher than I had ever heard.

'What happened that day? We knew that we would be apart for a while. What was it that suddenly changed everything?'

I ignored the challenge, and forged on.

'Then you were away in Vienna and your grandmother died. It gave me the chance I needed to bring things to a halt. I'm sorry how it came over. I really wanted to speak to you, not hide behind a voice message. Then, as things turned out, Richard was taken ill before you returned. It was such a bloody mess. He could have died. You surely understand that I couldn't let him to find out about us when he was so poorly.'

'And what now?' he asked, the tone of his voice slightly more measured. I walked over and stood facing him.

'Nothing has changed. I still feel this is wrong.' I searched his face for a glimmer of understanding but found none. My voice lowered. 'I hate doing this to Richard but I simply cannot continue without you in my life.'

For moments he stared into my face, showing no emotion. This was a new side to Benjamin, one that made me uneasy.

'So, this is what it will be? Meeting when we can.' I nodded.

'This is all it could ever be. We both knew that.'

He twisted away and gripped the rail of the Aga, his head bowed, giving nothing away.

'I still need to understand about our last time together. What was the tipping point?'

I turned to the worktop and swept the spilt grains of coffee into a neat pile.

'It was when you persisted in questioning me about the scar. I didn't want to talk about the baby I lost. Not to you. Mary's birth, her death was something that happened to me and Richard.' I twisted round to face him, seeking understanding in his eyes. 'Weirdly, I felt that talking about it was a betrayal. How mad to see that as more of a betrayal than falling in love with you.' My voice broke.

After a long pause, his face remaining without expression, Benjamin pulled me towards him, cupped my face with his warmed hands and kissed me hard, so hard it hurt. Relief flowed through me and I responded, crushing him to me.

'Upstairs?' he whispered as our kisses became more urgent.

'Not in this cold house,' I smiled. 'Far cosier down here and I've been fantasising about having you on that rug.' Was that really me? Did I suggest that? So this was my New Year.

*

The growing intensity of the *Adagietto* underpins her regret that she had allowed the affair to re-kindle. Why had she not listened to her instinct that led to their original break-up? To Georgina, this music represents not the deep ache of desire intended by Mahler, instead more the fundamental anguish of pain, the pain she experienced in losing Mary.

*

The horror of that morning will remain with me for ever.

'Tea for you.' Richard, ready dressed for work, stood beside the bed, a cheery smiley Jeremy in one arm. 'You've slept well. Baby gave you a night of peace at last.'

They wandered out of the room as I lay without moving, savouring the moment of relative comfort before the child within me would start its perambulations which included stomping on my bladder. So, before my tea, a slow lumber into the bathroom would be necessary.

It was as I put my feet to the floor that I first realised something was wrong. Instead of the gyrations of the unborn baby, who normally protested at a change of position, there was nothing. Just an unmoving solid weight.

Richard came running back into the room on hearing my frantic call.

'She's not moving. Something's wrong. She isn't moving,' I whimpered. From his bedroom came the wail of Jeremy sensing trouble.

'Surely that can happen sometimes?' asked Richard, trying to recall the ante-natal advice that had floated his way. Rationally, I knew he could be right but my instinct was not wrong. Despite Richard reassuring me throughout the journey to hospital, already I knew my baby, my little baby girl, was dead.

I heard the doctor's voice explain that, sadly, my baby had died and, given the closeness to my full term, they intended to induce the birth. Richard's white face mirrored my own horror.

The curtains surrounding the bed provided no privacy as I wept, Richard holding me close as his own tears fell. Neither of us could find words.

The next twenty-four hours were unreal, something to be endured. The induced delivery became complicated, ending in an emergency caesarean section. I could scarcely take in what was happening to me.

My mother came up to look after Jeremy as I recuperated from the surgery. As ever, she avoided discussing the emotions I felt. That was fine. It made it easier for me to cope.

We asked the family not to come to Mary's funeral. Richard took the tiny coffin from the undertaker and carried it into the chapel of the crematorium. We didn't go to church during those days in London so an unknown vicar read the funeral service. I felt devoid of feeling, as the curtain closed on the coffin, little Thumbelina encased in a walnut shell. Where did that thought come from?

The months after losing Mary were the emptiest of my life. I thought I would never emerge from such depths. Poor Richard knew I was suffering and simply didn't know how to help me. Instead he spent more time with Jeremy, implicitly reminding me that I should treasure what I already had.

In time, after I recovered from the caesarean, I sensed Richard wanted sex again. His approaches were tentative and so I chose to ignore him, even silently accusing him of trying to replace Mary with a new baby. That was harsh. He had his physical desires, as would I, just not yet. Very likely he wanted to express his love. I just didn't want him near me. It took some time before my hormones kicked in again and the desire for another baby returned and so Mark was born.

It hadn't been my intention to give Mark a name just one letter away from that of Mary. I certainly didn't regard him as a replacement for her and was only slightly disappointed to be expecting another boy.

Many years later, my mother was visiting us up in the North. The boys had been particularly raucous, which never bothered her, and that day I lost patience, especially with Mark. Even at a young age he developed the art of dumb insolence which riled me beyond belief. And he knew it.

Maman put down her newspaper and removed her reading glasses.

'Georgina, it is not Mark's fault that he is not a daughter.'

I stopped, iron poised over yet another shirt.

'What did you say?'

'You cannot resent Mark for not being Mary,' she shrugged in response.

'You are being ridiculous. A cruel thing to say.'

'It is the only explanation I have for why you always find fault with him. In truth he is no more naughty, difficult, than Jeremy. Enough, that is my view and it is for you to consider in your heart if I am right or not.'

With that the subject was closed although her words remained with me ever more. In time, I came to recognise the validity of her view. In doing so, I tried, tried so hard to overcome the negativity towards the boy that eventually I had to admit. Ashamed, I attempted to suppress my aversion. I didn't always succeed.

Undoubtedly, Mark was sensitive to my feelings and responded accordingly. How awful, to suspect your mother doesn't love you fully and unconditionally. Sadly, despite my efforts, a degree of reticence remains between us even now. His teenage years are proving truly horrendous. I seem to have lost any vestige of his respect and now it can only get worse.

*

She looks upwards to the high arching ceiling, away from the distraction of the orchestra, and she melts into the final part of the *Adagietto*, where Mahler laid bare his soul as he expressed love for Alma, the wife who would come to betray him, even though she remained with him to his dying day. For Georgina, this music always represents sublime sadness. It evokes the memory of a muted pink dusk over the Venetian lagoon beyond the silhouette of San Giorgio Maggiore.

Her gaze slowly returns to the auditorium and for the first time rests upon the people in the choir seats, only some twenty yards away. Her body turns to ice as her unbelieving eyes meet the cold stare of her son, Jeremy. She stifles a gasp as her attention is drawn back by a low moan from Richard, his face grey and bathed in sweat.

Chapter Eighteen – Benjamin's Story

The auditorium is silent. As the conductor eases the strings so, so gently into the *Adagietto*, the anticipation of the audience is palpable. The harpist's fingers flutter through the opening bars. Despite its familiarity, this movement never fails to stir Benjamin's emotions. Mahler's Fifth Symphony has been a constant thread throughout his life.

He is confident that, despite whatever has spooked her over the last few days, even Georgie will be affected by the *Adagietto* and, whether she wishes it or not, right now he is in her thoughts. Gustav Mahler has long held special significance for Georgina and she has often talked of the composer's marriage to Alma and the wife's subsequent infidelity. Although never openly referred to, the comparison between Mahler's marriage and her own is the elephant in the room. There are even parallels with

Richard's heart attack and the illness which ultimately led to Gustav's death. Does Benjamin see himself in the role of Gropius, the architect who loved Alma, stood aside while she nursed her husband, and ultimately married her? Hardly. Such commitment is beyond him.

Mahler's music draws him instinctively back to the world of his Viennese grandmother, and the slow pace echoes her final days as she slept her way to her God.

*

I felt vaguely uncomfortable as I sat in Oma's overstuffed sitting room in her small apartment down a nondescript side-street south of Karlsplatz. Slowly and with respect I sorted her personal effects. Each book, bundle of papers, album of photographs represented cherished parts of her life. It seemed like prying.

So little evidence remained of Oma's pre-war life and her escape into Switzerland. In a deep drawer I came across an old shirt-box printed with the name and address of a Viennese men's outfitters. It probably belonged to my grandfather, who died long before I was born. My father recounted how Opa was always well turned out, not easy in those grim post-war times when people scraped together a living. When did Oma choose this box to safe-keep her treasures? Perhaps after Opa's death, when she was left alone to raise my twelve year-old father and his big sister, Luisa. No wonder Oma became a tough old bird.

I was touched to discover the childish hand-drawn birthday cards sent to her from me and my sister, and between tissue paper there was a fragile, pressed dark red rose, its colour still remarkably true.

It was the bundle of letters that held my attention. From the stamps I saw they came from Switzerland. They were addressed to Frau Kellner, Oma, but the address I didn't recognise immediately. The franking mark on the top-most envelope told me when they were sent and I calculated that my father was around six at the time. Some fifty letters were tied neatly in fine string. I riffled through the pile and from the thickness of the envelopes estimated that each contained several pages.

I was about to call out my discovery to Pappi, busy in Oma's bedroom discussing with Tante Luisa whether to send all the clothes to a charity. I hesitated. Nobody should intrude into the past life of someone close, unless invited. Reading those letters would be like going through someone's diary, although I reasoned that she'd had loads of opportunity to get rid of anything confidential. Had she wanted the letters read? Some devious instinct, maybe founded upon my own dubious history, encouraged me to fold the letters inside a newspaper and slip them into my rucksack.

The evening spent over supper with Tante Luisa and Pappi seemed interminable. Vienna was suffocating in the summer heat and I itched to get back to my little hotel and satisfy my curiosity. I'd already worked out why letters to my grandmother might not be sent to her home address. Takes a cheat to know one?

My hotel lay in the same side street as Oma's flat and I sat in my room with the window wide open, the swish of traffic and the grumble of the trams passing the end of the road a constant reminder of present times as I studied a story of long ago.

The letters were arranged chronologically over four years. Good Austrian orderliness, I smiled to myself. They started when my father was two years old and my aunt four and ended when he was six. All were written in the same hand, each signed Ruedi.

From his first letter I gathered that Oma had taken her two children back to Switzerland to show them off to the family who had cared for her and her sister, Gabi, before and during the war. The address on the envelopes? Of course, the flat where my great-aunt Gabi had lived in the post-war years and beyond. I dimly remembered visiting her when I was a child. I never knew the name of the people who had become their adoptive family during those horrific years when the girls hadn't known whether their parents were alive, imprisoned, dead. My father would remember the family, of course. He had been part of the reason for that visit, a summer holiday, taken while my grandfather continued working in Vienna. They must have stayed several weeks in Switzerland. As I skimmed through the pages, the letters referred to excursions on the Vierwaldstättersee, rambling over the Rigi mountain, my father strapped to the back of his mother and Tante Luisa to the back of – Ruedi. Picnics with his family were fondly remembered, as were evenings spent walking alone with her by the lake. That was the factual side of the letters, the innocent framework from which something deeply wonderful grew, emerging more strongly with each letter.

With dawning understanding I scan-read the neat, rounded hand-writing. In deference to her, he wrote a precise *Schriftdeutsch,* high German, not the Swiss dialect she would have had to learn to speak within his family. During that holiday, away from my grandfather's eyes, they had become lovers. Or become lovers again? I read on, impatient to discover whether this betrayal by my grandmother was a *coup de foudre* or a resumption of something that had existed before she met Opa? I hoped for the latter. Somehow I believed that would mitigate the betrayal. Why should it matter to me whether she'd cheated on her husband or not? Who was I to judge? After all, wasn't I, too, having an affair with a married woman?

As I read on, I discovered that during those war years she and Ruedi had grown up together in neutral Switzerland, in a village shielded from the day to day terror of living as a Jew in Austria under Hitler's Reich. Nevertheless, life in this land-locked country was still a struggle for most, with food rationing and the ever-present fear that the Führer would fulfil his boast to pick up Switzerland on his way back home from conquering the rest of Europe.

The son of her guardian family, Ruedi was like a brother to her but during the seven years she had lived in their house, that must have changed. So why had she returned to Vienna? How old was she when she and Gabi took the train back to the city which had rejected them and thousands of other Jewish families? Why return? It had never been discussed among our family. Maybe my father knows and now, with her passing, will tell her story.

Unfortunately, these letters showed only one side of the correspondence. How did Oma respond? Over the four years, Ruedi's letters expressed a yearning that grew in intensity. Apparently he had never married and was working for a business near Lucerne. He plainly adored her but the early letters revealed a respect for her loyalty to her husband and her intention to stick by him, even though their life was a struggle financially. Shamefully, I couldn't stand the suspense and after devouring the first ten letters I jumped ahead to the last three. She had returned to Switzerland in the third year of the letters. Again with the children. Again without Opa. She had gone back to say goodbye to Ruedi, to bring it to an end. She hadn't replied to the penultimate letter and probably not to the last, dated six months later. From these last two letters I sensed Ruedi's distress rise from the page.

Did I admire Oma's steadfastness? Was she distraught in bringing the affair to a close? Was she consumed with guilt or had the futility of the affair caused it to wither and die for her? After all, why didn't they get together after Opa died only six years later? Even before Georgie's voice-mail message the following morning, I felt the stirring of doubt in my own life.

*

The mood changes and in the *Adagietto* Benjamin hears a pleading female voice, which descends to pitiful desperation before rising again, insistent in its cry. The conductor's face mirrors the anguish as he bears over the violins and draws them to his will.

*

The supplicating voice could equally be that of a man. Ruedi? Maybe Oma had moved on from him, found reconciliation within her own marriage? The attraction of an illicit lover must have been especially strong for a woman, still young but dragged down by two children and a shortage of money in post-war Vienna. Yet even illicit affairs can time-out if the substance isn't there.

Is that where I am with Georgie or is there something more sinister behind this latest cold shoulder? Has Richard found out? We were so careful. Surely Jeremy wouldn't tell her that he's gay, about him and me. Except there is no him and me. Just a one night fumble. Something I wish had never happened. Worst of all, he's now become so bloody clinging, so fucking needy.

'Hi Benny, only me. How're things? Did you get my last message? Had a really crap day – all lectures, no playing. When can you get down again? Call me.' And so it went on. I left it days before I responded, aware that he'd get wound up, just as I get wound up from not seeing Georgie.

Early in January, I had some free days coming up when his latest call hit my voicemail.

'Hi there.' The exuberance in his voice leapt out of the phone. 'I've checked your schedule.' Why the fuck did I ever give him a copy? 'Gergiev is here with the Marinsky and I guessed you'd be up for it, so why not come down for a couple of days and we can hang out? Let me know soon. The student tickets are like gold-dust.'

His voice slipped into that irritating hesitancy: 'Hope you can make it Benny. I've missed you ...' His voice tailed off and the line went dead.

I pushed the decision to the back of my mind. It would be a great concert to hear. It's years since I've had the chance to hear Gergiev and his band but did I really want to continue this whole stuff with Jeremy? There was no doubt in my mind that it would be easier to cope with the break from Georgie if I had little or no contact with her family.

I texted back a bald response: *Sounds good. Need to check other plans first*. Keeping my options open.

Next day was a rehearsal day and by lunch time I was totally pissed off by the visiting conductor who possessed zilch communication skills and was struggling to impose his own interpretation of the Brahms planned for later in the week. I walked to the shopping centre ostensibly to find a sandwich but really to get out for some fresh air, albeit amidst a cold grey winter's day.

As I queued in Prêt to pay for my sandwich and smoothie, I gazed out at the blank people huddling down the street, heads bowed against the bitter wind.

'What the hell. I'll text him after I've eaten. Gergiev wins hands down. As for the rest ...'

I headed back to the rehearsal hall. My mobile signalled the arrival of a message but I ignored it until I was back in the warm and had hung up my scarf and jacket. I found a quiet corner and unwrapped the sandwich before fishing out my mobile.

In urgent need of tuition. Free next Wed, Thurs, Fri. Let me know. G

I was stunned and gazed at the message, lost in thought.

'Bad news?' asked one of the trombonists. I shook my head, closed my phone and focused on eating the sandwich which now I could barely taste. The rehearsal continued within ten minutes and during the next two hours I tried to think only of the music.

I was still angry with her but at the same time I wanted to see her. What did she have in mind? Belatedly I realised that any of those days would prevent me travelling down to hear the Gergiev concert, but what did that matter?

After I reached home I sent: *OK Wed. Usual time?*

I texted Jeremy: *Sorry, can't do Gergiev. Thanks, B*

*

There was snow on the ground in the higher villages and as I pulled into the drive of Greystones, it crossed my mind that my tyre tracks would reveal that Georgie had received a visitor. I swiftly forgot the indiscretion as the apprehension and excitement that had swamped me over the last few days surfaced again. Despite my anger, I wanted to be with her. I wanted to make love to her. But I wanted an explanation.

I lifted the violin and music cases from the boot and stood in the porch, stamping snow from my feet as I awaited a response to the door-bell.

There she stood. Her face looked more strained than before and she seemed thinner, despite the thick navy jumper and flared tweed skirt. I guessed this house costs a fortune to heat in winter.

'Benjamin, how lovely,' was her polite, almost embarrassed welcome as she took my things and indicated the kitchen. Its warmth hit me as I entered and I walked over to the Aga to warm my hands. Gloves are essential for violinists in winter time and I'd walked out without them.

As she fussed with the coffee mugs, I sought to break the ice:

'So, here we are. Again?' She nodded but said nothing. I struggled to keep my voice level. I was trembling, perhaps with anger, perhaps with anticipation, but I deserved an explanation. Did she really think I'd simply roll over for her? Why had she cut me off?

She kept her back turned as she tried to excuse herself, explain her guilt over cheating on Richard. I walked over to the window in frustration. I didn't buy it. I wanted to shout at her that she'd understood from day one what she was getting into. As I stared out over the bleak garden, the shrubs indistinguishable, smothered in snow, I heard her pour water into the cafetière, releasing the seductive aroma of coffee. Hesitantly she defended Richard and claimed that things had changed after our last time together in the summer.

Enough of this crap. I spun round, wanting to shake her. Instead I held back and returned to the safety of the Aga, gripping the towel rail hard. I tried to control the fury in my voice but I had to discover why the fuck she'd dumped me just with a phone message.

'What happened that day? We knew that we would be apart for a while. What was it that suddenly changed everything?' She seemed not to hear my questions, or chose not to. Her excuses came tumbling out. Evidently, Oma's death served her purpose pretty well. Gave her the out she needed. Then came her apology for hiding behind the voice-mail.

Spineless, I wanted to hiss at her. I focused instead on my distorted reflection in the lid of the hotplate before me.

Then she dealt the argument without contest: Richard's heart attack or whatever. So why the fuck am I here now? Is she desperate for a shag? I turn to face her, keeping my tone even.

'And what now?'

She crossed the kitchen and stood close, so close I felt the warmth of her body. I breathed in her scent. I wanted her and despised her at the same time.

'Nothing has changed, I still feel this is wrong, I hate to do this to Richard but I simply cannot continue without you in my life.'

So I'm to be the occasional fuck, I seethed internally.

Evenly: 'So, this is what it will be? Meeting when we can.' She nodded, claiming that this was all we could ever be. I turned away from her, fearing I might slap her. Madam High and Mighty bestowing her favours. She who pays the piper ... Well, if that is how it is to play out, so be it. But on my terms, lady.

I wasn't prepared to let go and repeated my earlier question.

'I still need to understand about our last time together. What was the tipping point?'

She stood with her back to me, messing with spilt coffee.

I never would have guessed that it was the dead child that lay behind her decision. Yes, a dreadful thing, but some twenty years ago. Surely enough time to come to terms with it. I didn't buy that bullshit about revealing to me something very personal to her and Richard. What's more personal than making love to another man's wife? Trumps everything in my book.

Her dark hair fell forwards, masking her face. My anger was undiminished. She says she can't live without me but she doesn't want emotional commitment either. Fine, that suits me too. From now on, new rules. Enjoy it while it lasts. Getting emotionally involved was never the intention. Complicated things.

As for Jeremy, I pushed thoughts of her son to the 'deal with later' corner of my mind.

Facing Georgie, I showed no emotion. She was uncertain of my reaction. Good. I would not be wrong-footed by her ever again. I would be in control from now on.

As I kissed her lips, she drew me down onto the rug at our feet, the warmth from the oven relaxing us as we urgently undressed and roughly took from each other on the hard floor. At that moment, I believed I would always be in control.

*

The tenderness of the *Adagietto* builds into deep passion, Mahler's passion for Alma. After today, Benjamin will never again hear this music without feeling betrayal and hatred. His bow caresses the strings of his violin and the scant sound feathers, floats away and is gone.

For now, though, he welcomes the conductor's briefest pause between movements before plunging into the final *Rondo*.

Let's get today over.

Chapter Nineteen – Jeremy's Story

The girl has checked her messages and returned the phone to her bag. Her crassness enrages Jeremy and he glares at her. Tears of anger, tears of frustration, gloss his eyes. Will the *Adagietto* bring him solace from his nightmare?

He closes his eyes to block out the girl, his parents, Benny. He breathes deeply as the violins float into his consciousness and he sits back, uncaring that tears slowly escape his eyelids or whether the girl beside him notices.

*

Could that message on Dad's phone be from Mark? He's in town tonight with mates. Maybe he's after a lift home with Dad rather than travel back with Mum. You couldn't call him a hypocrite. He doesn't attempt to disguise his lack of respect for her. I couldn't work out why, but since Sunday I totally get it.

Over Easter there was a mega bust-up between them. I came into the kitchen half-way through the row, by which time Mum was well steaming.

'It's not much that I'm asking, Mark. Just tell me in advance when you're going to need picking up from town. I have my own life, too, and it's a busy one.' She glanced up from the worktop where she was rolling out pastry, looked at me momentarily and dusted flour from her hands. Standing there in jeans and t-shirt, she revealed how much weight she'd lost and for the first time I noticed real tension lines in her face. Mark was slouched in an easy chair, eyes and fingers focused on some game on his phone.

'Mark, answer me when I'm speaking to you.'

He made no response, calmly finished the game, unfurled from the chair and headed for the door. Mum darted forwards and physically restrained him, her floury fingers marking his navy sleeve like corporal's stripes. He stopped and turned to face her. He's pretty well fully grown now and stands a couple of inches taller than Mum.

'Don't imagine I don't know what's going on,' he hissed and, with a look of utter contempt, shrugged her hand away and left the room. Embarrassed on Mum's behalf and struggling at what to say, I wandered out of the room, leaving her standing in the middle of the kitchen, her floured palms held away from soiling her jeans, as in supplication. Her face paled.

I followed Mark up to his room where he sat in a swivel chair beside the window, his laptop already switched on.

'Why do you behave like such a prat with Mum? She fusses too much sometimes but she could be a helluva sight worse.'

He continued to set up a game and spoke without raising his eyes.

'You have such unquestioning faith in people, don't you? You think you understand people inside out, especially when you live with them. But, you see, you never know the real person. There are always secrets. Little secrets and,' pause for dramatic effect, 'fucking big secrets.'

'What secrets? Has Mum got secrets?'

Mark smiled bleakly: 'Ah, that's my secret. For now.'

He refused to reveal anything further. I felt cold. Had he discovered my secret?

*

Jeremy opens his eyes. He focuses on the ledge where his parents sit and watches his mother lean towards his father, placing her hand over his. Jeremy cynically views her expression of tenderness. With the dying notes of the *Adagietto*, Jeremy remembers the concluding scene of *Death in Venice* as the failed Aschenbach in his final agony gazes across the sands to his dream disappearing in the silver light.

Jeremy shudders.

Chapter Twenty – the Girl's Story

The girl relaxes. From the text message, she gathers that the dice are cast. The hall is still. With a hardly perceptible gesture from the conductor, a sound, soft almost to silence, emerges from the violins. The woman playing the harp extends graceful arms and plucks out an overlying tune. Even the girl is arrested by the beauty of the music. It reminds her of some movie seen but no longer remembered. Like the soundtrack to a romantic tragedy.

She steals a sideways look at the guy beside her and is curious to see tears slowly coursing down his cheeks.

So your life's shit, too.

*

There's not been a load of romance in my life. Even the thing at uni with Ned could hardly be regarded as a romantic affair. For him it was a shag and someone to prop up his essay writing. Not sure what it is about me and relationships; they don't seem to go anywhere. Mind you, the majority of guys I've met aren't worth hanging onto anyway. They say a girl is attracted to a man that reminds her of the best bits of her Dad. How would I know? I suppose the only male role model I've had is The Bear. Not that he would fulfil my dreams by a long stretch.

Tim is probably the closest I have to something worth hanging onto. Crazy to believe that. I've years ahead and the last thing I need is to be bogged down with a guy at this stage. So much I want to do. Travel, earn loads of money, meet interesting people.

Travelling out to site with Tim, I got to know him better. We had much in common.

'Dad died when I was thirteen. Don't suppose there is any right time to lose your father but Mum struggled to fill the gap, emotionally as well as financially.'

'Not having a Dad around meant that I expected nothing as a given,' I responded. 'Made me grab whatever was going.'

Although we'd shared pub lunches while out on site visits, it wasn't until last week that he invited me out for a drink after work. Saddo that I am, I believed, hoped, that he fancied me. He's quite fit, after all.

'You seem to get on well with the boss.' The statement, really a question, rankled. Was he having a go, digging for dirt? Not an innocent remark.

'I make it my business to get on with people I work with. Don't you?' I batted back.

'Can't help noticing you've had some run-ins with the admin girls ...'

So, that's where this was going. There'd been an unpleasant spat a couple of weeks ago when Miriam, queen bee in Accounts, had made pretty pointed remarks about my expenses on the trip to the Midlands with the boss. She'd worked out that I hadn't claimed anything for dinner and that his chitty claimed for two. She'd been with the company for ever and had known his wife so felt protective of her memory, perhaps. Or was just plain jealous.

'Looks like you were treated to a posh dinner up in Birmingham,' she announced to all and sundry as I passed her desk. I should have let it go but that really isn't my style.

'And your problem is?'

Her response was a dismissive shrug. However, the damage was done. People knew we had gone up north together, but not why. This cow was implying he'd taken me with him for a shag. That's what lay behind Tim's question.

'What are they saying about me?' I confronted. Give him his due, Tim didn't beat about the bush.

'The word is that you're having an affair. I just wanted to give you the heads up.'

'And do you think I am?'

He looked me in the eye: 'No.'

*

The girl is struck by the rapt attention of the audience. Nobody coughs or fidgets. She wonders why so many of the musicians sitting with hands folded in their lap have their eyes fixed on the sheets of music before them.

If you're not needed for this bit, why not chill and watch the world?

She decides that this is the best bit of the music so far, even though it's really, really sad. The guy beside her has closed his eyes. His cheeks are now dry.

*

The meeting was held in the boss's office. Tim and Hussein were already seated, mugs of coffee before them, and they looked surprised to see me. The PA looked daggers as I passed her desk and closed the door, excluding her. Something was going down.

We were on the acquisition trail and this was the war party. Bloody fantastic. In at the beginning. I crowed about it to Mum that night.

'He's been looking at businesses for some time and he's going for one in his home town.' Mum looked up from her paperwork.

'Oh yes? What sort of business?'

'It's run by a guy he knew in his first job and again in London. Maybe you met him?' After all, it was in London that Mum first met The Bear. She responded with a non-committal movement of the head, neither yes nor no. Not interested.

Nonetheless, as the deal developed, Mum would enquire on progress, almost out of encouragement than real interest. Strangely, she never asked about it when The Bear came round, when she could have had chapter and verse.

Something grabbed her, though, when I admitted that we had a mole in the other camp. One of the guys was feeding us information.

'You mean he's revealing the financial situation of the business?'

'Sure, and who they are dealing with on the client side. We've picked up some real gems.' Mum nodded thoughtfully.

'Does this mole aim to get a leading position if the deal goes through?'

'Too true. The plan is to get the deal through then boot out the guy who owns the company. His business is rocky and he'll be glad to get out.'

'I'm not so sure,' she mused. 'People who run their own business tend to be pretty tenacious. It's not just the money at issue. It's been their child, what they've nurtured. There's pride and status too.'

'I'm sure we'll make him an offer he can't refuse.'

With a bitter smile she replied: 'Not if that offer is made by Tony Mulligan.'

Meetings with the other team were held half-way between offices to keep the deal under wraps. The guy didn't want to spook his own staff and risk defections.

I first saw him about a month ago at a hotel in the Midlands, just off the M6. He was quite tall, with sharp features, similar age to The Bear. His thick, brown hair was receding slightly and starting to go grey. He wore rimless glasses, which slid down his nose. I suppose not bad looking in a studious way. He made it quite clear that the merger wasn't his first choice and wasn't on his agenda. We knew otherwise. There was a pathetic bravado in his approach. We played along. It was like a cat playing with a mouse. Didn't particularly want to kill it, just terrify it. The man talked a good talk yet we knew the business was about to go tits up. He was pathetically arrogant.

'Will he put up much of a fight when it comes to it?' queried Mum.

'He might have done but our insider has provided us with the winning card. He's been bribing a planning guy in some local authority up there,' was my triumphant beat-that explanation.

'Are you certain?' What a strange question of doubt. Why wouldn't this pompous Mr Do It My Way not bribe someone? What did she know?

*

Two weeks ago, The Bear called round home. We'd not seen him there for a while and I wondered whether he wanted to talk through with me the final stage of the deal, due to be settled this week. Mum seemed to have been expecting him.

Instead of his usual banter, he walked straight into the lounge and we followed on. He stood in front of the TV and we sat facing him, I wondering what the hell was to come.

'Your mother wants me to tell you something. Right, Mel?'

This was it? He was going to tell me that they are moving in together. I felt a smile rise to my lips.

'It's time you know the identity of your father.' They both studied me for a reaction.

'O-Kaaaaaay ...' was my guarded response, my hint of a smile disappeared. 'Why now?'

Not the response they expected.

'Because there's a meeting next week and it's important you understand the context and implications.'

Context? Implications?

'Next week I plan to finalise the deal to acquire the practice of Richard Johnson, a deal which will bring great benefit to me and my business but a deal which is likely to ruin him. Richard Johnson is your father. You can work out the implications for yourself.'

*

The music is painfully slow like an old woman feeling her way across a room of memories. The orchestra plays softly, scarcely a sound, before building speed and intensity, just as tears form then overflow in a stream impossible to stem. The girl looks across to the ledge. The man's wife is leaning over to him, her hand clasping his.

Sweet, thinks the girl sarcastically. In truth she envies the gesture of affection as the strings sob ever more gently into silence.

** FIFTH MOVEMENT *Rondo Finale***

Chapter Twenty-One –

Richard's Story

The conductor ploughs straight into the final movement but Richard is oblivious to the music. He squeezes Georgina's hand in a half-hearted attempt to allay her concern. He feels desperately weary, totally drained. Bed is where he wants to be right now. First he needs to return to his office to erase those computer files, the ones that would reveal just how much he'd paid out for that girl. If Melanie plays dirty, he could end up handing over his business to Mulligan and losing his wife as well.

*

Everything is such a lash-up. Even at the birthday party something felt wrong. I can't put my finger on it. On the day of the party, when she was supposed to be looking forward to a slap-up family dinner, her behaviour was weird.

She walked through the back door mid-afternoon, hair done up more elegantly than usual.

'You look great.' And she did. Her smile of thanks was fleeting. She looked distracted.

'Look what's come for you.' I pointed to the massed bouquets from friends and close family. We'd lined them up on the scrubbed kitchen table, awaiting her choice of vase and position around the house. She bent low over the flowers, inhaling the perfume of roses and lilies, murmuring her appreciation.

'There's one from the orchestra too,' pointed out Jeremy. 'Bet that was Benny's idea.' Benny? Since when has he been Benny? Either way, Georgina seemed less than enthused. Strange. She disappeared upstairs into her study and I saw nothing more of her until we met up in the bedroom, each preparing for the 'celebration meal'. If she suspected something more elaborate, she gave nothing away, yet I detected an uncharacteristic reserve which she sought to mask with slightly forced enthusiasm.

At the end of the evening, we prepared for bed. The tension was almost tangible. Her gaiety during the party, her effusive thanks as we were driven home, all sounded brittle to my ears. I'd wanted so much to make the evening special and forced to the back of my mind what the do had cost. A bit like the London Olympics, planned before the financial crash. If I'd realised before I sent out the invitations that my business would be going belly-up, no way would I have pushed the boat out this far.

Even the boys were odd over the weekend. Mark was Mark, but even more annoying, whereas Jeremy transformed from his usual Tigger bounce on the day of the party into the foulest mood on Sunday morning. To everyone's surprise, he headed back early to uni, catching a mid-day train, instead of the first off-peak service yesterday morning. What was that all about? He had no exam until today.

*

The music switches mood, becomes more challenging, goading, the taunting voice of Mulligan. In the quickening pace, Richards detects a call for flight.

He weighs up the odds. What's the point of fighting Mulligan? Either way, the business will be lost. Better to go with dignity and salvage something, than have to call in the receivers. He stares blindly towards the musicians, his thoughts ricocheting. If only he could wrap things up more neatly.

He is alerted by the insistent vibration of another message to his phone. This time he doesn't hesitate. The pace of music, together with the vigour of the conductor and orchestra, hold the attention of the audience. He again draws the phone from his pocket, ignoring Georgina's supplicating look.

Caller unknown. Message: *It's time to meet. I'll find you after the concert.* For the second time he sits stunned. Conscious that his breathing has quickened, he inhales deliberately and slowly before returning the phone to his pocket. Without looking at her, Richard senses Georgina's anger.

*

Who the fuck is it? Mulligan? No, his name would appear on screen. Who else? Someone from the practice? Why no name?

Melanie? Why would it be? I'm getting paranoid. Is she up here after more money? If so, I'll soon put her straight. No ... more ... money. That's it. Over. Her problem now.

Christ Almighty. One mistake, one mistake over twenty years ago and I'm still paying for it. For her. For a child ... for the daughter I didn't want. Not then.

*

As he casts about for answers, his eyes meander up beyond the orchestra to the audience seated in the cheap choir seats, more brightly illuminated than the rest of the hall. His gaze is arrested by a strikingly dressed girl. He takes a moment to identify her out of context and without her usual glasses, but then he recognises the dress and the wearer: Sarah, Mulligan's PA. He watches her. She rests her chin on her hand, her elbow propped on one crossed leg. He is struck by this stance, by a resemblance. Who does she remind him of? He continues to stare at her hunched figure as he trawls through his memory. Of course, that's how the young Melanie would sit on a bar stool, way back when. Her features aren't really Melanie's, though there's something about her that recalls the slender young woman who once enticed him.

He is uncertain but the girl seems to stare right back at him. Mesmerised, Richard returns her gaze. Slowly the question forms: could she be one of Melanie's children?

Mulligan could still be in contact with her even after all these years. Is it possible that he's given her daughter a job? She could be Penny's sister. This is Sarah. Penny's in a wheelchair with MS.

The girl turns to face the person on her right and to his shock, he now looks into the eyes of Jeremy, and even at this distance, he sees angry eyes. In an instant his stomach clenches with realisation then fear. They are here together. That's it. Jeremy has discovered all about Melanie's daughter, his father's daughter, Penny. Sarah must have told him everything.

How long has Jeremy known? Richard's breathing quickens again as his thoughts fly. Is the lad so bitter for his mother's sake that he'd connive with Mulligan to gain vengeance? Is that why Georgina has been so distant? She's found out.

Wild suppositions skim through his mind. Jeremy knows nothing about the business nor about the Amberley weekend. It can't be him feeding Mulligan.

As Richard's eyes flick between his son and the girl, his horror intensifies. There is a strange resemblance, one with the other. It is the jaw-line. His own distinctive jaw-line. They could be siblings. He draws deep for air.

She isn't Sarah, she's Penny. She has to be my daughter. But Penny has MS. Penny is in a wheelchair for God's sake.

Richard's breathing becomes increasingly laboured and he glances back at Georgina only to see her looking beyond him towards the choir seats where she, too, has spotted her son. Her eyes are swimming again with tears as she turns to look at Richard.

Georgina does know. Christ, she's found out everything.

He feels his chest will explode with anger, with grief. And with pain.

Slowly Richard slumps sideways in his chair, leaning heavily against the shocked woman beside him. At once Georgina is out of her seat trying to pull him upright, away from the now concerned woman. He hears Georgina whispering his name urgently. She is trying to help him but he worries that they are in full view of much of the auditorium.

Don't make a fuss, it will be all over very soon.

The music, at least.

The orchestra powers away, oblivious of what is happening above the players' sight line, its concentration firmly on winding up the emotions for the stately finale. But for much of the audience there is now another focus of attention.

Richard is vaguely aware of Georgina holding him steady. Her perfume accompanies the massive pain. He feels exposed and cold yet the sweat is pouring off him. Although the music is much louder now, sounding like the peal of bells, he hardly hears it. He is terrified.

This isn't supposed to happen. Not yet. It wasn't like this last time. Not pain like this. Is help coming? Everyone will be watching. Georgina, help me. He slides in and out of consciousness just as the music races away to the finale. Through the roar of applause, he hears Georgina's reassuring voice. Something about Jeremy here. But it's too much to bear and he slips away again.

Chapter Twenty-Two –

Georgina's Story

With hardly a pause the conductor moves into the final movement. Georgina scarcely hears the music as her attention fixes on Richard. He closes a clammy hand over hers and smiles, a bleak hopeless smile that ices her heart.

Might he also have spotted Jeremy? Guilt over-runs her. Was Richard expecting him? Are they planning to confront her afterwards? But not here, surely not here? If anywhere it would be at home, in private. A confrontation here would also involve Benjamin. She cannot believe that Richard would do such a thing; it would destroy his reputation too. Or doesn't he care anymore? In any case, didn't Jeremy's message say specifically that he wanted to talk without his father present?

She attempts to reassure herself; maybe the deal with Mulligan is going badly? The lesser of two evils.

*

Mulligan has been a thread throughout Richard's life, woven subtly, hardly visible, but occasionally surfacing to create a fault in the fabric of our lives. Something serious happened in those early days while we all lived in London. Something involving the two men around the time of our wedding. I never reached the bottom of it; far too wrapped up in wanting to be married, to have babies. No feminist, me.

After returning to the UK from Geneva, I'd been involved with somewhat rackety types, certainly none that I'd take home to meet my parents. Richard's more grounded approach to life had an appeal, especially as I began to consider life ahead and the possibility of children. Friends who had married in their early twenties now had babies and although weariness featured prominently in their lives, I envied them.

Richard was quietly ambitious and I could see that he intended to make something of his life. He soon made it clear that he wanted me to be part of that life. Occasionally I met some of his colleagues and the one that stood apart from the others was Mulligan, not only because he hailed from the same town as Richard. I didn't care for him. He had no finesse and it wasn't difficult to detect the antipathy between the two men.

Now Mulligan has the whip hand. They talk of merger, but what if in reality it is Mulligan taking over our business? Richard would hate that. It meant so much for him to return from London, build a successful practice and become a man of substance in his home town. He would loathe working for Mulligan. He just couldn't do it. Is that what's stressing him?

I'm not much help either. Just when I should be supporting him, just when he should be able to talk and share his concerns, that's when I've been totally wrapped up in Benjamin, physically and emotionally. I suspect Richard isn't being totally honest with me, not wanting to worry me. But who am I to talk of honesty?

My wake-up call came during the half-term holiday this spring. Mark brought home a school-friend whose parents live abroad. Jack was to stay with us for the week so it meant giving up my study-cum-guest room. The week beforehand, Benjamin managed to get over to the house twice, aware that we couldn't meet during the boy's visit.

As we lay side-by-side after love-making, hands clasped, our eyes were drawn to the signs of spring's arrival, the delicate pink leaves pushing through on the massive copper beech, sentinel outside our window.

'So, a house full of adolescent testosterone next week?'

'It won't be so difficult. Jeremy will have his head down working for his finals and Mark will want to get out and about with Jack. I just have to run them to the bus in the village and they'll get back later in the day, no doubt ravenous. I've loads of food in the freezer so catering will be simple. And it's always good to have someone new at the supper table. It stops the boys bickering.'

'When does Jeremy get back?' How casual the enquiry, but no doubt he already knew.

'Saturday morning and he'll come with us to the concert that evening so you'll have the chance to say hello during the interval maybe?' He gave a non-committal shrug.

'He keeps on about inviting you down to the Birmingham concerts.' Again an unspecific reply. Instead he rolled towards me and brushed his lips over my nipples. I stretched, arching my back ready again to entwine my legs around his.

So quickly turned on. So easily seduced into believing that what we had was love. Was it really love or sheer lust? If love, how misplaced. To love a bastard who could switch so easily from me to Jeremy and back again. He disgusts me.

Would I have been equally disgusted had he moved on to another woman? Do I loathe Benjamin because he's bi-sexual? Is my so-called tolerance of homosexuality simply the veneer of liberal thinking? Below the surface, am I as homophobic as Richard?

It was the day after I drove Mark and Jack home from school that Mark's attitude deteriorated further. I didn't notice at first as my focus was on Jack settling in.

'Did you sleep well, Jack?' The two boys were demolishing a cooked breakfast long after Richard had left for work, despite it being a Saturday.

'Brilliantly thank you.' He exchanged a look with Mark. 'It's a great bed, really big.' He beamed a smile at me. I smiled back enthusiastically, moving on to the plans for the day, in happy ignorance.

Mid-morning my mobile buzzed with a text from *Annette*, my pseudonym for Benjamin.

'Have I left my hall pass?'

I felt sick. If he had dropped his smart-card to get back-stage at the concert-hall then it lay somewhere in the room where Jack was staying. The boys had taken off on bikes an hour earlier and weren't due back until lunch-time. I ran upstairs and pushed open the door into my study, now transformed into teenage chaos.

Think logically. Where would Benjamin have dropped it? From his trouser pocket? From his jacket pocket? The chair where he normally draped his clothes was not in its usual position. The card was nowhere obvious and in any case I would have noticed it when preparing the room for Jack's visit.

I dropped to my knees and slid my hand under the bed, probing backwards and forwards until my fingers touched the smooth plastic. His card, his card with his name and photograph. Under my bed. Far under my bed. I could hardly breathe. It couldn't have fallen that far under. Just under, perhaps, but not that far under. Someone had found it, retrieved it, read it, grasped its meaning, replaced it but not exactly where it was found. I started to tremble as I realised the implications. Was it Jack who discovered it? Had he shown it to Mark? Had Mark realised how the card came to be in my study? The comment about the big bed. The glowering looks from Mark all morning. He knew.

If he did, nothing was said. The holiday ended and both boys returned to school but I awaited the Easter holidays with trepidation. Would Mark choose that moment to reveal his discovery? Or would he wait? Knowledge is power, as Richard always spouts. The Easter break came and went, again without a confrontation. I reassured myself and Benjamin that we'd got away with it. He brushed the matter aside, past history as far as he was concerned.

I was already stressed ahead of my birthday party, suspecting, quite reasonably, that Richard would plan something bigger, as a 'surprise'. But nothing prepared me for Jeremy's bombshell the day before. The morning of the party, I sat at the hairdresser's, parrying her inane chatter as I strove to get my head around the situation. I'd hardly slept the previous night and longed to doze as she soothingly blow-dried my hair. I was disgusted and revolted. The thought of Benjamin doing unspeakable things to my son filled me with horror. Images, horrendous images, refused to be blanked from my mind.

Then the party and warm reception from friends and family as I moved around with a drink before we sat down to eat. I guessed what was to come. I'd spotted Benjamin's car at the far end of the car-park and I worked out that he had been invited to perform, maybe with other players.

Conscious that the birthday girl's reaction would be observed, my face was frozen in a rictus of delight as we all listened to the mercifully brief recital. I felt trembly inside as Richard and I walked over to the players to thank them. As I reached Benjamin, convention dictated that I should kiss his cheek and as we drew apart I regarded him with all the loathing of my being and, with satisfaction, saw his eager smile dissolve into blank confusion. *Message delivered, Benjamin.*

My only concern now was that Jeremy should not discover my affair with Benjamin and that Mark kept his suspicions to himself. When early on Sunday morning Jeremy departed, unusually dark and withdrawn, I wondered if Mark had revealed something, but I couldn't work out when they might have talked. Jeremy had gone to bed after the party, fizzing on a high, and next morning announced his departure way before Mark emerged. Inexplicable.

*

She risks another look towards Jeremy. His eyes are focused on the musicians. Watching Benjamin? As the music picks up pace she glances at her husband. Such a pallor. He really doesn't look well. Should she persuade him to leave now, before the music ends? Suddenly Richard stiffens and she sees his hand feel in his jacket pocket and withdraw his phone, on silent but flashing. She beams her supplication: *please don't.* His desire to see the message outweighs her disapproval and again he drops the phone under cover of the programme to read the display.

Georgina sees his face sag as he stares at the screen. It must be a short message as he immediately slips the phone back into his pocket. Initially he stares bleakly out over the auditorium then he turns back towards the orchestra. Has he seen Jeremy yet? She cannot follow his line of sight but she steels herself to look over to her son whose gaze is now fixed in her direction but she cannot be sure whether he is looking at her or at his father. Either way, Jeremy's face is grimly set.

She spots the brightly dressed young woman seated next to Jeremy and there is something about her that is familiar. The girl ignores the orchestra below, her head turns towards Jeremy, then she looks over to where she and Richard sit. Georgina cannot decipher the girl's expression and leans forwards better to see her husband's averted face. *Is that girl with Jeremy? Why does she appear familiar? Is she something to do with Richard?*

The music reprises Mahler's theme but now she is incapable of losing herself in its compelling flow. Instead she continues to regard her son and this woman. Where has she seen her before? Bizarrely she has a look of Richard's sister, Tricia, the same family jaw-line. She's young, around Jeremy's age. A bit older than Mary would have been. She tries to stifle a thought before it takes hold, but too late. She feels the tears begin to well in her eyes. Ridiculous. This cannot be. She stares hard to make the tears evaporate.

The girl turns her head again to Jeremy but he doesn't appear to respond. *Are they together? Who is she? How does Jeremy know her?*

Richard turns back to Georgina as his breathing becomes ragged. He falls away from her against the woman beside him. In panic, Georgina slips onto her knees, trying to drag him upright, away from his neighbour, wanting to help him but without causing a commotion as the symphony draws towards its climax.

The man seated next to Georgina whispers: 'I'll get help.' As the audience breaks into rapturous applause, he disappears into the corridor.

Georgina is now on her feet, cradling Richard's head to keep it upright, but unsure of what to do. Put him in the recovery position? She looks over to Jeremy. Whatever has gone before, she needs him now. The audience continues to clap as the conductor highlights individual players who have excelled. With relief, she sees Jeremy step roughly over the knees and bags of people in his row but is puzzled when the girl follows close behind him. Fleetingly she reflects that they are together.

A man approaches, another concert-goer.

'I'm a doctor, shall I take over?' he states rather than asks. Thankfully she steps back and shortly a first-aider appears, dressed in a high visibility vest. Georgina stands a little apart, not taking her eyes off Richard's wax-like face as the two men bend over him.

A suited administrator joins her and whispers reassuringly that paramedics are on their way. She stands with her back turned to the applauding audience, conscious that she is in full view now, as is the group huddled over Richard.

'Please God, don't let him die. Not now. Not here. He doesn't deserve this.'

Jeremy appears at the top of the short flight of steps down to their seats and deliberately pushes his way past the vacated chairs. He stands just above his father. He doesn't speak, just watches the activity of the doctor and first-aider.

Georgina is conscious that he gives her not one look and her tears brim over and flow down her cheeks. Groping in her handbag, she removes a folded handkerchief. She looks to the top of the steps, willing the paramedics to be here and notices the girl surveying the scene without emotion. Her vivid dress echoes that of Georgina, mocking the grimness of the moment.

Turning back to Richard, she sees his eyes open.

'Richard, darling.' His immediate recognition of her is encouraging. 'Jeremy is here too. The ambulance is on its way and you'll soon be fine, don't worry.' His eyes close again and her voice falters. Some instinct causes her to turn and spot Benjamin at the top of the steps, violin in hand. *Not you, not now*, she wants to scream at him. *Leave us alone.*

As Benjamin turns to leave, his way is blocked by two people. One is Mark, here for his lift. He runs down to his father, ignoring his mother. Georgina looks on helplessly. *Please, not now. This is when we all have to pull together.*

The second person is a bulky figure who pushes past the violinist. She is astonished to recognise Tony Mulligan. He surveys the group surrounding Richard but turns to the girl in the pink dress and they move to one side, talking in low voices.

Confused, Georgina turns away, away from these outsiders, away from her lover, her boys, her focus for now on her husband.

Chapter Twenty-Three –

Benjamin's Story

Benjamin rests his bow across his knees as the leader of the horns opens the final movement. Only at bar 62 do the second violins dash into the mêlée and Benjamin's fingers fly over the strings, spiriting his instrument's unique sound.

*

Oma discovered my violin two years earlier when clearing the apartment of a dear friend, and offered it to me when the orchestra was performing at a concert in Vienna's Musikverein.

'What's the history?' I guessed that the woman who had recently died was also Jewish and that undoubtedly there would be a story.

'Ilse's father was a violinist who taught the son of a wealthy family during the years leading up to the war. The boy, an only child, was given a valuable violin from the beginning. A ridiculous indulgence,' Oma sniffed. 'He adored Ilse's father and under his tuition made good progress. When the boy fell sick and died, his parents were destroyed and gave the violin to his teacher so that he might instruct children from less fortunate homes. As things became more dangerous for the Jews, Ilse was sent away to safety with the *Kindertransport* and the violin was packed among her possessions, possibly as a means of raising money. She never saw her parents again. The precious violin she never sold and now I have it here. There is nobody else to take it.'

I handled the violin. So much tragedy, yet this instrument of beauty survived.

'You would like me to have it?'

'Of course. It must be played again. To honour Ilse's father and the boy that died.'

*

Through the depths of winter and the awakening of spring, the sex with Georgie was frequent and good. For me though, the relationship was now on a different level. More like my past encounters. Good sex, no emotional entanglement.

During our first months together last summer, I was totally besotted with her. It wasn't just the physical side that I relished; Georgie had style, a surprising sense of humour. I let down the barriers and responded to her generosity of spirit. I should have spotted the danger.

Apart from the fact that she was good in bed, I couldn't help but like her. She never said a harsh word about anyone, even about Mark who could be a little prick.

Mark constantly gave her grief. She talked of his dark hints, but about what? I never told her of the time he'd unexpectedly answered my call to the house phone during our 'off' period. Did he suspect us? I advised her to keep her nerve.

She was concerned that over Christmas Mark had spent some days working with Richard's book-keeper. Had he discovered her mobile phone bills, which would have revealed her long calls to me in Vienna last summer? If he had, he would also have noted that the calls ceased thereafter. I dismissed her fears as the consequence of her guilt.

That aside, following what she likes to call our *rapprochement* early this year, I became more wary of our relationship. I forced myself to observe our coupling in a detached, more analytical way. How does she really see me? As her toy-boy? The age difference is significant. But surely, a toy-boy is there to be flaunted, whereas our affair has to be totally secret. Georgie is terrified of discovery.

Which is why I hesitated to call her about my hall pass. Normally fixed onto a tape hung around the neck, these credit-card size passes provide Open Sesame to backstage at the concert hall. My tape had worn through and I hadn't replaced it. I would slip the card into my wallet or violin case, sometimes carelessly into my trouser pocket.

That Friday afternoon, when I couldn't lay my hands on my pass for the final rehearsal, the hall staff waved me in. Later I rummaged the flat, searching everywhere for the bloody thing. Where and when had I last carried it? Then I remembered. Shit, for Thursday's morning rehearsal, after which I'd driven up to see Georgie for our last meeting before the boys came home for half-term. Christ Almighty, had I left it there? If I had, surely she or the cleaner would have found it after making up the bed for Mark's schoolmate? And she would have texted.

Have I left my hall pass? was my simple message which would be announced under the name of *Annette*, a female name which would raise no comment if someone picked up her mobile.

Half an hour later she rang.

'I found it under the bed.' I felt a wave of relief, quickly dashed by her voice, taut with fear. 'Right under the bed. No way did it fall there. Someone has found it, read it and thrown it even further under the bed.'

'You're imagining that,' was my less than convincing response.

She ignored me: 'The question is, whether it's only Jack that found it or Mark as well. You should have heard Jack's comment at breakfast about enjoying his 'really big bed'.'

'That's still no reason to believe that he has guessed or that Mark knows.'

Georgina spoke honestly for the first time: 'Mark is foul most of the time but this morning he hit the depths and looked at me as though I was dirt. And of course he's right.'

'Oh for God's sake.' I wasn't prepared to take this melodrama. 'Look, don't try to return the card, just cut it up. Security will deactivate the code, give me a new one and fine me seventy-five pounds. It's my own bloody fault.'

'What if Mark tells Richard?' Her question hung in the air. What the fuck to say?

'You're leaping ahead, Georgie. You're not sure whether Mark has found out or not, and from what you've told me about his general attitude, I reckon the little shit will bide his time and then use it to get something out of you, rather than go to his father.'

That was a step too far. As soon as I spoke I knew I'd said the wrong thing.

'We'll speak after the holiday.' She ended the call.

*

'Has anything been said?' I opened the first conversation since the boys' half-term holiday. Her voice down the phone sounded tense but slightly relieved.

'Not a thing. The week went by OK, nothing out of the ordinary, i.e. Mark was Mark, Jack was polite and actually quite good company. He made us laugh. And Jeremy was subdued, I suppose he's got his finals next term so he's focused on his studies. He said he tried to contact you a couple of times to meet up, but no joy.'

'Mm, I've been busy with stuff and meant to call him back,' I evaded. 'How about meeting up this week?'

And so we picked up as before. Each week up until Easter we would meet at least once, not making any big thing out of it. After all, the last thing we wanted was for the family to demand a recital out of our master-classes.

I feared my guard was beginning to fall. I wrestled with the dilemma: is the attraction the regular illicit sex or do I again have deeper feelings as during those early days? Keeping the relationship at a purely physical level would reduce the emotional involvement, which I found disturbing, disruptive. The reality is that she offers me much more than sex. This dangerous enchantment could destroy my life if I let it happen.

*

The showdown I feared came over Easter. On Good Friday, we were due to perform *St Matthew's Passion* to a capacity audience. Georgie planned to bring her parents and in-laws plus her two sons and, of course, Richard. Ahead, I warned her that it was unlikely that I'd make an appearance front of house before the concert. Afterwards I was racing for a train for the holiday weekend with my folks. It would also avoid an awkward meeting with Jeremy who was nagging that I hadn't travelled down to stay with him.

I checked my phone just before switching it off for the duration of the concert. A message. A number I didn't recognise. A weird but explicit message:

Amazing how phone bills mount up with overseas calls to Vienna. Could be expensive on many levels. We should talk. Mark.

I felt sick. Georgie had worried her calls to me last summer would show up on her mobile bill. Mark had been working with the company book-keeper and had probably uncovered her phone history.

Call to platform. Nothing to do now. Throughout the oratorio, I felt Mark's eyes on me with their implicit threat.

As I wedged onto the crowded train to Birmingham, I was mystified by Mark's intention. The implicit threat was to reveal his mother's secret, but what did he expect in return for keeping stumm? Surely, he realised that musicians earn sod-all, so he can't be blackmailing me for money. Did he want me to end the relationship, so protecting his father's position? That would take some explaining to Georgie without revealing her son's involvement. Or, did he want to put the screws on his mother, in some way to get back at her? But why? What has she ever done to Mark?

I returned north on Easter Monday. Mark would be home until the next weekend.

We met at a nondescript pub in town.

We arrived separately and bought our own drinks. I had found a banquette some distance from the few customers in the bar.

'So Mark, you wanted to meet.'

He sipped his lager then leant back hooking his thumbs into the waistband of his jeans. He is so unlike his mother and brother, yet doesn't resemble Richard either. He bit his bottom lip and threw a challenging look at me.

'Have you told her you're meeting me today?'

No point in prevaricating. 'No.'

'Funny, at first I thought you had the hots for my big brother. Didn't realise your sights were on my mother.' I ignored the remark, intended as an insult, and took a swig of beer. What was his point?

'You called the house one day last autumn when I happened to be home for a dental appointment. I called the number later on the off-chance. It went to your voicemail. Why was our violinist friend phoning the house when normally only my mother would answer? So, I kept a note of the number. Then at Christmas I had to help out at my Dad's place, checking invoices. I found all these calls to your number, from my mother's mobile. Long calls. Overseas calls. More than you would expect from a patron, surely? So, I decided to become more observant and thanks to my mate, Jack, all was revealed. Well, your pass at least. Under the bed in my mother's study. What a surprise.'

'Get to the point Mark.' This young puppy was getting on my tits.

'The point? You want to get to the point?' He smiled but without warmth.

'Next year I'm due to go to uni. My parents expect me to go to uni. The last thing I want to do is to go to uni. Instead, I want to use the money for three years of travel. To travel wherever in the world I want.'

'Trouble is,' he shrugged mockingly, 'the family would be horrified and no way would they agree to it, especially as my Mum's parents would be footing the bill. So here's the deal. My beautiful, honourable, upright member of the community, mother will persuade my Dad, but more importantly, her parents, to stump up for the travel.'

'Or else ...' I led him.

'Or else her reputation is up shit-creek. Everyone, but everyone, will discover she has behaved like a tart. Not sure what the orchestra would decide for you. Maybe it's what musicians do?'

I wanted to hit him, hit him hard. Fucking prick.

'That's a hell of a lot for your mother to achieve. There will be huge resistance from all sides, even if she agrees to do it.'

'There'd be a hell of a fall-out if she doesn't,' he replied with quiet menace.

'What do you think will be her reaction when I put your proposal to her?'

He shrugged.

'Look, the timing for this is crucial. Within the coming weeks we have her fiftieth birthday, your Dad's surprise party for her. Do you want to screw that up or can it wait until after then?' I had to gain time. The last think I wanted was for the shit to hit the fan before then. If she is presented with Mark's demands now and agrees to get his travel funded, or, more unlikely, decides to face the flak, either way, that party would be an absolute charade.

In retrospect, I see the irony of all this. I tried my best to protect her for that party, the point when she froze me out.

'OK,' he conceded. 'But I want it sorted by the end of the summer term. I am not going on to uni. Understood?'

I walked to the bus stop, my head pounding with Mark's demands.

*

The build-up to last weekend's party was difficult. Richard and I spoke on the phone about Georgie's birthday party and secrecy was the watch-word. Secrecy indeed, on all sides. Mark's threat of exposure lurked at the back of my mind.

An excited text came from Jeremy. *Gr8 your playing at mums party. Perhaps u can come down to Brum soon. J.* I ignored it.

And then we had Saturday night's performance. I still don't get it. Georgie and I had been together as usual on Thursday. Jeremy and Mark were due home on Friday for what she expected to be a family dinner the next day to celebrate her birthday. I blanked out thoughts of blackmail and although she hated the prospect of becoming fifty, she was looking forward to being treated by 'her boys' as she called them.

I slipped from the rumpled bed and dragged over my worn leather music bag.

'I've a present for you.' From the depths I pulled a gold coloured envelope.

'Thank you,' was her automatic but excited response as she tore it open. Her face brightened but still questioned what lay in her hand. Then she guessed and pulled me close. Her kiss said everything.

'OK? I've got the partner ticket to this, so are you up for a weekend in Vienna to see *Tosca*?' It was risky to expect her to escape for a weekend without Richard, but I guessed it would appeal and somehow she would find a way. I guessed right and my gift was rewarded enthusiastically there and then.

So what the hell changed between Thursday and Saturday night? Had Mark decided after all to screw up her birthday by telling Richard about us or by threatening her that he would do so? Hardly the first - Richard would have cancelled our gig rather than see me there.

Saturday night I was too angry to sleep after she blanked me at the party. Instead I lay in the dark playing loud music through my headphones until the battery failed. Whatever the reason, she didn't have the decency to tell me to my face. Now I was stuck with two opera tickets, which cost a bloody fortune. And what about Mark's threats? I'd had enough of this fucking mess. I'm out.

By five a.m. I'd had enough of lying there, my head spinning with disconnected words and jumbled thoughts. I sat up and in the light of dawn tapped into my phone my message to Georgie.

What the fuck was last night about? I play you our love song then you walk over and treat me like dirt. Georgie this is the last time. We are done.

I pressed *Send*.

*

His arm aches as the violins race, sweeping joyously upwards towards the finale, only for the brass to cascade notes like a cold shower. Benjamin looks up fleetingly. In his sightline, beyond the conductor, he is aware of movement. He continues a few bars more and looks again, this time focusing on the ledge. Georgie is kneeling, her arms supporting Richard. Shocked, Benjamin stops playing and gazes up at them. As

Mahler's Fifth Symphony helter-skelters down to a rousing end and the audience breaks into applause, he watches the man next to Georgie speak briefly to her then run up the steps.

The lights go up. Georgie is standing now and gives way to another man who leans over Richard. Benjamin is rooted to his seat, partly because at this point he cannot get up and walk out, but also because he is unsure what to do. Despite better judgement, his instinctive concern is for Georgie coping alone and he determines to get off stage the minute he can. The conductor turns on the podium to acknowledge the enthusiastic applause and then one by one, section by section, indicates the stars of the symphony to stand and take their bow.

Benjamin cannot take his eyes off the group up on the side ledge and is aware that, despite the fulsome applause, many of the members of the audience are also watching the action above. He is surprised to see Jeremy appear at the top of the steps and descend to stand just above the group administering first aid. He supposes Jeremy has attended the concert to meet up with him afterwards, as his text indicated. Benjamin strains to see Georgie's reaction. Why hasn't Jeremy gone to his mother's side? Why isn't he comforting her as she delves into her handbag to retrieve a handkerchief?

He starts to doubt. Have both Georgie and Jeremy discovered his relationship with each of them? Is that the source of her anger and the reason for Jeremy's request to meet? Shit, shit, shit. How could that be? Surely Jeremy hasn't told her?

The conductor takes his third bow and departs. As the applause diminishes, some people head for the exit. The orchestra leader stands, violin in hand, bows to the audience and leads the players from the stage. Benjamin suppresses the instinct to get the hell out of the place and instead crosses the stage to exit by the far door, a faster route to reach front of house and the ledge where this drama is playing out. Whether or not he will be welcome, he just knows he has to be there.

Battling up the back stairs, he emerges through a security door. People he recognises as hall management cluster around the archway onto the ledge. They turn at the sound of his running feet and show mild surprise to see a musician in full orchestra dress, sprinting down the corridor, bow and violin gripped in his hand. He pushes through and pauses at the top of the steps, out of breath, taking in the scene. The first-aider and the man in a suit are bending over Richard. Georgie is speaking to her husband. Jeremy stands apart, intently watching. A blond girl stands near Benjamin. Almost as though he emanates a radar signal, first Georgie then Jeremy turn and regard him.

Georgie's face is not welcoming and Jeremy's contorts into a frown of anger. *Shit, bad call*, he thinks and turns to leave. Two people appear at the top of the steps. Mark runs down the steps, acknowledges his brother, blanks his mother and peers forwards to see his father. The second person is a short, middle-aged man in a double-breasted suit who pushes past Benjamin, pauses and takes the blonde by the arm, steering her to one side.

Benjamin hesitates. Stay or leave. On such small decisions, lives are changed and, despite his better judgement, he remains and watches.

Chapter Twenty-Four –
Jeremy's Story

The calm opening of the final movement does nothing to allay Jeremy's fear. He follows the dialogue between soloists: French horn, bassoon and oboe. Their curious exchange gives way to voices of other instruments. The second violins remain silent and he looks down to where Benny focuses on the score before him, awaiting his next entry, apparently isolated in the music. Jeremy knows otherwise. Each musician is ever mindful of the rhythmic beat of the conductor and depends on each other to perform their best.

Jeremy's face sets grimly, recognising the fallibility of trusting others. Within days, hours, the actions of those you trust can turn life one hundred and eighty degrees.

*

The party was to be the one high spot of a term of revision and exams. Dad thought it would be great to surprise Mum with a celebration and I knew there was a chance I'd get to see Benny at some point, albeit fleetingly.

On the journey home last Thursday I decided that this could be the right moment to tell Mum. About me. About me and Benny. I was so sure she'd understand. I'd let her be the judge whether to tell Dad. That would be more difficult. Ironically, the one thing that made me apprehensive was telling her about Benny. How sick was that? Next day I waited until Mark disappeared with mates and I had her to myself. We ended up in the garden, enjoying the rare afternoon sunshine and I listened to her prattle on about her music appreciation group before I butted in.

I built up to it slowly, explaining how I knew I was different, even at school. She frowned and I could sense a tension. So I came straight out with it.

'Mum, I'm gay.' She made no movement, said nothing but continued looking at me, showing no emotion. I couldn't read her reaction but, as it wasn't one of horror, I continued. What came next seems so bizarre, knowing what I do now. I burbled on, explaining how things got easier at uni without the hot-house pressure of boarding school and then I actually told my mother that the best thing that ever happened to me was meeting Benny and becoming his lover. Benny, my lover. Her lover.

I totally misread her response. She rose from her seat and walked away a few steps. She gazed out over the flower beds to the fields and beyond to the moors. I carried on talking, believing that she was simply giving me space, and explained that Benny hadn't always been gay and in the past also had girl-friends. As I spoke, I felt the tears well up in my eyes and my voice faltered. Immediately she turned and in a moment was on her knees hugging me.

'Oh my love, my poor love,' she whispered in my ear as my tears of relief finally flowed. 'It's been hard for you to carry this alone. Everything will be alright. Just remember, Jeremy, you are you. And I love every bit of you.' Did she honestly mean that when she said it?

She paused and looked me in the eye. 'I think it's probably best if we keep this to ourselves just for now. No need to tell Dad yet. He has a lot on his plate with the business and it might not be the best time.' Another pause: 'Does Mark know? About you being gay? About Benjamin?'

'I think he guessed some time back, even at school, Mum, but he has never said anything. And as for Benny, nobody knows about him, just you. I don't think the other players are aware either. We are very careful.' Being careful is something Benny is good at. Only just not enough this time.

That was it. I was out, only out to the wrong person. She hid her feelings superbly but the next day, the day of her party, she wasn't her usual self. She seemed flustered as she walked in from the hairdressers and her reaction to all the flowers struck me as forced. When I pointed out the bouquet from the orchestra, I suggested that perhaps it had been Benny's idea. She nodded without the enthusiasm I'd expected. I concluded she might feel ambivalent towards him now, as her son's first lover. Wrong. She was simply trying to control the same anger and sense of betrayal that tear me apart now.

*

The music develops into a wild country dance and Jeremy returns to the present. He cannot believe his eyes. The girl beside him is writing a text, shielding her flying thumbs from the view of the audience behind her large handbag, now perched on her lap. Outraged, he nudges her arm. The girl looks him full in the face for the first time. He frowns and shakes his head. She shrugs, quickly completes the message and despatches it into the ether.

Couldn't she bloody wait? The concert's nearly over?

He continues staring at her, his anger for Benny and his mother channelled at this girl. Eventually she turns to him. Her gaze is disconcerting. Not because of the frank challenge in her eyes, but because there is something familiar about her. Has he met her before? Is she the sister of someone from school? Whatever, she's out of order, seriously out of order.

Among the orchestra, the storm mounts. The woodwind and brass protest vehemently, the strings fight back. The symphony will end soon, bringing closer the confrontation with Benny, then with his mother. His attention returns to his parents and, to his disgust, he sees his father lean to one side as he retrieves his phone from his jacket pocket. Even from the choir seats, Jeremy sees his mother glare at his father.

What is it tonight? I've never seen people this blatant in a concert.

Whatever the message, it has affected his father. Richard stares out over the audience. He looks towards the choir and at first Jeremy fears his father might spot him. Instead, still angry with such crassness, Jeremy raises his head and glowers at his father. Maybe Dad isn't looking at him but instead at the girl beside him. Had he spotted her texting?

Out of the corner of his eye, Jeremy is aware of the girl looking at him. He ignores her, furious with her, furious with the whole world. He focuses on the ledge and is startled as his father appears to look directly at him. Jeremy flushes for all the reasons that trouble him: all the guilt and secrets. He is six years old again.

*

Dad, if only I could talk to you. You're the only one I can trust. You're probably the only one that doesn't get the fucking mess your family has created. I trusted Mum and she betrayed us all. I trusted Benny and he shafted all of us.

I now know why Benny was so on edge at Mum's party. He definitely dissed me when I spoke to him, then cut as soon as the recital was done. Too risky having both lovers in the same room, I guess, even for a skilled liar.

Dad, poor bugger, was oblivious to the whole thing. At home he laid on loads of booze in the drawing room, anticipating that quite a few friends and family would come back after the dinner. Instead, guests melted away around midnight and we were driven home. Despite Dad's hearty attempts to party on, it all fell a bit flat so everyone headed for bed before one o'clock. I'd drunk enough but, unlike Mark, well within my limit. On Sunday I needed to revise. Monday I'd take the train down to Birmingham.

Which is how I came to be up really early on Sunday morning, less trashed than the rest, I guess. The kitchen was littered with presents, still pristine in birthday wrapping, discarded coats and Mum's clutch bag. As I poured my first black coffee of the day, her phone beeped, announcing the arrival of a message. *Someone's keen to get their thank-you in,* I thought and, leaning across the kitchen table, I pulled out the phone to see who was the early bird. The name displayed was unfamiliar to me, *Annette*, but the start of the message was revealed and caught my attention.

What the fuck was last night ...

My curiosity was stirred. What sort of girlfriend would write like that to Mum? I stroked the open bar to reveal the full message.

... about? I play you our love song then you walk over and treat me like dirt. Georgie this is the last time, we are done.

I sat rigid as I battled to understand who lay behind the text. Annette? These weren't the words of a woman. I strove to find another answer, a more palatable answer, but suddenly it hit me. It could only be one person. Among the four musicians at the party only one person knew Mum well enough to call her Georgie. I clicked on her contacts and under *Annette* recognised the number.

I didn't want to believe what lay before me. Benny was texting Mum under a disguised name. He's been in a relationship with my mother, screwing my mother. And me. I could scarcely breathe. Tears flooded out. I buried my head in my arms on the kitchen table and sobbed. Sobbed with hurt, with anger. At Benny for betraying me and Mum for betraying all of us.

I had to get out of there. The phone lay on the table where I'd dropped it. The smoking gun. I slipped it back into Mum's bag. She would see that the message had been opened and I left her to guess who had read it. I really didn't give a fuck anymore. I tore a sheet of kitchen roll and blew my nose.

I retrieved the phone again from her bag. Think about this. Don't be too hasty. If she's unaware that this message has been read, she'll think her secret is still safe. In fact, even better, if she never sees the message at all, she won't realise that Benny has dumped her.

In which case, what's her next step? Surely she'd want to have it out with him. She wouldn't just walk away, not when her lover has two-timed her, especially with her son. After time to calm down, perhaps she'd invite him over to Greystones for another of their 'coaching' sessions, believing that she's the one in control. Not this time. If Benny did agree to meet her, might he guess that Mum had uncovered our relationship?

But what if, after she calms down, she still loves him, forgives him? What if she doesn't confront him and wants their affair to continue? I couldn't bear that.

It was a no-brainer. I had no option. I deleted the text. Let her find out the hard way that she's been dumped.

By the time I'd showered and packed, the family were gathering for breakfast, Dad in charge for a traditional

Sunday morning fry-up. Despite remonstrations and offers of hang-over remedies (my puffy eyes), I pleaded the need to return to uni and got a lift off a mate to catch the mid-day train south. My farewells were less than gracious and I could hardly look Mum in the eye. She smiled at me uneasily, unclear as to what lay behind my sudden departure.

I sat on the train and looked out over the folding-in moorland and indifferent towns. I had fallen out of my world.

*

Jeremy's eyes are riveted on his parents and he watches Richard turn his head away from the stage to look at his mother. What does his father know? Has she told him that his son is gay to deflect attention away from her own sins? He suspects his father's reaction. He has heard the condemnation of 'shirt-lifters' often enough.

His despair swerves into sick horror and he gasps as his father slips sideways and ends up draped over the woman beside him. His mother's reaction is fast and she slides from her seat to kneel on the floor, half hidden by the balustrade as she tugs at his father's jacket to pull him upright.

French horns are held high and, with drum roll and cymbal clash, the symphony has reached the closing bars. Jeremy cannot wait. He picks up his bag, crouches and climbs first over the bare legs of the startled girl beside him, then past the others in the row, variously indignant or furious at this lout ruining the end of their favourite Mahler symphony. He ignores the hissed criticism and leaps up the short flight of steps which take him into the connecting passage towards the ledge where his father lies. Half-way down the corridor, amidst the roaring applause, he hears the sound of running feet and turns, expecting a stream of abuse from the steward who barred him from the first half. Instead it is the girl, the girl in the pink dress, who has followed him out.

Ignoring her, he continues, stopping at the opening onto the ledge where management types are clustered. At the top of the steps he pauses momentarily, conscious that there are some two thousand people seated in the auditorium, most of them applauding enthusiastically at the performance just ended, but many of them also with eyes fixed on the small group leaning over his father. He slowly descends to a level just behind the high-viz jacket of the first-aider and sees his father's ashen face. He is conscious of his mother's presence but cannot look at her.

It's all your fucking fault. See what you've done. Where's the ambulance? Where are the paramedics?

He looks over his shoulder in anticipation and is startled and even more annoyed to see that the same girl is now standing in the doorway, blocking the access. He urges her away with an angry gesture and she stands to one side, quietly eyeing the scene, betraying no emotion.

Bloody ghoul. Why are you here?

But his attention is drawn back to the kneeling man in a smart suit who is talking to his father. Jeremy cannot hear his words as the audience continues to applaud the conductor back to the stage for the third and final time.

Reluctantly he looks at his mother, standing slightly apart from the group but watching intently with tears streaming down her face, her hair in disarray. She reaches into her handbag for a handkerchief and retrieves a square of neatly ironed white cotton, which swiftly becomes soiled with mascara and make-up as she dabs below each eye. He hasn't seen her cry like this ever before. He is discomforted.

The huddle closes up and he cannot easily see what is happening. In that moment the orchestra starts to stream from the stage, left and right. One person pushes against the flow. Jeremy sees Benny weaving among his fellow players to exit on this side of the stage.

Surely he doesn't plan to come up here? That's the last thing we need.

He watches the first-aider and the man in the suit start some procedure with a piece of kit which Jeremy assumes is for a heart attack. He still cannot look his mother in the eye but is aware that her attention is drawn to someone over his shoulder. He turns to see Benny breathing heavily at the top of the steps. Jeremy frowns angrily at the violinist who turns, as if to leave, then pauses as first Mark then a portly man in a business suit enter. The stranger looks about, spots the girl and joins her.

Jeremy flinches inwardly as Mark's gaze sweeps him without emotion. Despair overwhelms him. Where is the warmth, the love within his family? He turns to face his father. Maybe it lies there before him, at imminent risk of expiring for always.

Chapter Twenty-Five –

The Girl's Story

Without pause, the conductor conveys the orchestra from the powerful sorrow of the fourth to the wistful awakening of the fifth and final movement. The girl continues to observe the man and woman, their hands touching.

That's what I never had from you, no touch, no cuddle, no pat on the back. You just paid your money and walked away from any responsibility. And yes, how you have paid. Thousands over the years. No more than I was due.

*

That morning, when they told me Richard Johnson was my father, I felt I was being tested. After the revelation,

Tony sat down next to my mother, perched forward on the edge of the settee, elbows on his knees, his fingers paired in a loose steeple pointing at me. He was no longer my Bear. His penetrating eyes searched for my response.

I was shocked and looked at Mum who frowned anxiously.

'Penny, this has come as a surprise, but Tony didn't want you to be influenced during the deal process, especially as it will mean that the payments will surely stop, no matter how hard I threaten. He simply won't have the money anymore.'

I rose and walked over to the window, looking out over our small suburban garden to the backs of small suburban houses beyond. It wasn't the money I minded, it was him. Richard Johnson, my Dad? I didn't want him to be my Dad. I'd met him, not been impressed by him, not even liked him. Pompous prick. Not what I wanted for a Dad.

Suddenly I got it. I spun round and faced them both.

'How could you?' I hissed at my mother, pointing at the man beside her. 'How could you let him use me like this?' She was taken aback and began to speak. 'No, Mum, you hear me out. Do you think that this is all about a take-over bid? Just an astute business deal? Think about it Mum. Why does he want to take over Johnson's company? Think where it's located. Johnson's home town, and,' I gestured, 'his home town. If the deal doesn't go through, Johnson's business will fail. And yes, if it does succeed, he'll be out on his neck. His partners have been collaborating with us and are sure of that. He will lose his business and his position, not just in his professional life, but also in his home town. He'll be wiped out.

'So no, it's not just about the deal. It's about destroying Richard Johnson. It's personal. What I don't understand is why? Has the money he paid out for me also been personal? The tens of thousands he's paid us since I was born.'

Mum began to protest but I cut in.

'It seems to me that from day one Tony has been pushing your buttons to get money out of him. Behind it was always the threat of disclosure, telling his wife and family that he had a bastard daughter at the other end of the country. Maybe you never would have told her, but the opportunity was always there, Mum.'

She dropped her head into her hands while Tony sat gazing ahead, not at me.

'So was this all about vengeance? If so, on whose part? I've no love for the man, for how he disowned me, so was vengeance yours, Mum, or yours Tony?' He didn't flinch a muscle and remained silent as I turned on him.

'Your final twist of the knife came when I was eighteen and I suddenly developed an expensive medical condition. Whose idea was that? Yours, Mum, or yours?' He stared back at me with pursed lips and expressionless eyes.

'The money was certainly essential to get me through uni, I don't question that, but did we have to do it that way? You have to really hate someone to use emotional blackmail. It's only now that I get it.' I turned back to the window.

Tony cleared his throat and spoke to my back, using the voice I've heard him use at the office when he's telling staff how it is, how it's going to be, like it or not.

'You're wrong, Penny, and you're mixing two separate issues: first your right to demand maintenance from him and second, the fact that his business is failing. Vengeance has nothing to do with it.'

I walked over to my mother. 'In that case Mum, why do you still hang on to that letter written to you long before I was born. I found it years ago at the back of your dressing-table drawer. It was from you, Tony. I read it. An angry letter and I didn't really understand why Mum would want to keep something like that. You told her that she had to make a choice to be with you or with someone called Richard. I never knew who Richard was and, because I'd been snooping, could never ask Mum. Now I do know. She chose Richard over you and although in time you forgave her, you never forgave him. That's why you wanted vengeance.'

'Interesting,' Tony raised his eyebrows and sat back into the settee. 'You still have my letter, Mel? Must have meant something to keep it all these years.'

He opened his arms expansively and smiled at us both.

'Well, we are where we are. Whatever has happened in the past, two things remain: Richard Johnson is your father, like it or not. Other than financially, he has not acknowledged you throughout your life and has made no attempt to show interest in you. That in itself is enough to make me despise the man. What's more, he has enjoyed a good life, helped a lot by wealthy in-laws, and as far as I'm concerned, if his business is badly run he deserves to lose it. My vengeance, as you call it, is merely to have him face up to his responsibilities. He owes you that at least.'

He leant forwards and continued. 'I have a proposal.'

My urge was to walk away but just as my mother was caught in his web of power, so it seemed was I. He talked quietly unveiling his final plan, a plan which would guarantee the satisfactory completion of the deal. Yes, there was a degree of blackmail, but Johnson would see there was no alternative way out. He'd have to sign or his good name would be lost as well as his company. Maybe even the police would take an interest in his dealings with Saddlethwaite. But there was a further layer to the deal, one held in reserve and this was of greater interest to me. He would have to acknowledge me as his daughter, willingly or not. For me, this was beyond vengeance and I was up for it.

*

Today's opportunity only cropped up a couple of days ago. I'd given up trying to fix today's meeting by email and resorted to the phone.

'Yes, that would be fine,' Richard Johnson's PA confirmed. 'It's the only day that's clear, but he will need to leave at six for an evening engagement.'

'A business dinner?' I ventured, nosing into his private life.

'No, he's going to a concert with his wife. It's been in the diary for months. They're very involved with the orchestra so he won't want to miss it.'

His wife. She'll be with him. In public. Crazy thoughts raced through my mind.

'Fine,' I concluded. Absolutely fucking fine.

A scheme was developing in my head. Tony already had one plan but this would top it nicely. Initially, he wasn't sure but listened further then agreed with a thoughtful smile.

From the city's website I discovered what was playing and managed to get tickets. Single tickets were all that remained high up in the grand tier or in the choir seats, but that was cool. We wanted to be discreet and separate. From my seat, I might get a view of Richard Johnson, ready for our final move.

*

Penny surveys the orchestra. It's getting more than a little frenetic with all the instruments trying to jump in on the act. With no attempt at discretion, she looks at her large-dial fashion watch in anticipation that the concert will end soon. This is the moment. She lifts her capacious handbag onto her knee and slips her hand inside, feeling around for her mobile. Using her bag to hide the phone from the audience, she swiftly keys in a message. A nudge to her arm interrupts the flow and she glances at Mr Grumpy. He glares and shakes his head. *Tough.* She continues and presses *Send* before returning the phone and bag to the floor. His eyes are still on her and she returns his gaze, this time full on.

As the music burbles along she returns her attention to Johnson. Has he received her message yet? *Yes!* She watches as he pulls his phone from his jacket and hides it behind a programme to read the text. *That's really pissed off his wife*, she smiles to herself. Penny tries to gauge his reaction as he tries to work out who sent the message. *That's put a spike up his arse.*

From his seat on the ledge, Johnson looks over the audience and then towards the choir seats. She is pleased when he spots her and his gaze lingers, staring straight at her. She looks back. He must recognise her. The dress is distinctive and the one she wore to today's meeting.

She is aware that Mr Grumpy also has his eyes fixed on the ledge. Does he know Johnson, too? Suddenly he gasps and she follows his gaze to discover that the man has slumped down in his seat.

What the fuck?

Simultaneously, Mr Grumpy grabs his bag and without a word of apology clambers over her legs, scuffing her shoes as he goes. Everyone in the row reluctantly shifts legs sideways to make way, angry to have the final moments of the concert ruined. She looks back to the ledge where the wife is trying to help Johnson.

This is going to screw things up totally. She scowls. Instinctively she also takes the chance of escape. Feeding off the high energy blasting from the musicians as they race towards the finale, she grabs her own bag and follows. Oblivious to concert-going etiquette, she doesn't bother to apologise as she tramples over bags and coats. She speeds up the steps, unsure of the geography of the place but heading roughly towards the ledge.

I need to speak to him. That's the whole point of tonight. To tell him. Tell him who I really am. What I am.

Show him how he's been conned all these years. Taken for a ride by Mum. Make him hurt. Squirm in front of his lady wife. Pay for the years Mum struggled on her own. Pay for not being a proper Dad.

The music ends with a loud slithering rush, immediately followed by enthusiastic clapping. She sees Mr Grumpy running ahead of her down the corridor. He turns at the sound of her heels on the wooden floor but hurries on. To her surprise, he shoots onto the ledge where the man has collapsed.

Maybe he's a first-aider?

She stands in the doorway and regards the scene. Despite the continued applause and the orchestra still on stage taking their bow, most of the people in the surrounding seats have withdrawn, leaving the huddle bent over Johnson. Her neighbour stands back and watches. *What's his interest in this?* He turns, notices her and gestures rudely for her to move away from the entrance. She obeys.

Where has she met him before? Some time ago. At uni? Dredging back into her memory and within the context of the concert hall, it dawns on her.

He's the guy studying violin, one of Ned's friends, that pigging weekend up north at his parents. Must have been somewhere around here.

The wife looks no longer at her husband but at Mr Grumpy, who studiously ignores her. She starts to weep and dabs at her eyes with a proper hanky. Penny is unmoved.

Yes, a bit of pain in your life won't do any harm.

Apart from Tony's message earlier, the plan is not going well. They both want to confront Johnson in the foyer, in front of his wife and others besides. What's more, they need him fit to sign the deal tomorrow.

She moves further onto the ledge but away from the group and looks up towards the Grand Tier which is emptying quickly. She receives a text message.

What's happened? I'm on my way. She responds: *He's collapsed.*

What now? Is he doing to die? She's aware of his recent heart problems. Would that be a good thing for the deal? Easier to negotiate with his wife and the two partners who are already on side? But no, she doesn't want him to die. Not yet. She wants him to know. To know about her. To realise he'd paid thousands over the years, he'd been tricked. Above all, she wants recognition, contrition. Not his death.

One of the musicians enters the ledge, a violin and bow in his hand. He hesitates and stands back, watching the people hovering over the man. The woman and boy feel his presence, look up at him then twist away, clearly not pleased to see him. *Weird?*

The violinist turns to leave but hesitates as newcomers arrive. A teenage boy stands at the top of the steps, close behind him Tony Mulligan. She gestures for Tony to join her.

She looks to him for guidance.

EXIT

Chapter Twenty-Six

'What now?' asks the girl.

Mulligan shrugs off her impatience.

'Is he conscious?'

'I can't tell from here.'

'No worries. It's happened before, he'll be fine.' He looks towards Richard's hunched figure. 'Well, we'd better get on with it then.' Mulligan adjusts his cuffs, drapes a possessive arm around the girl and together they cross over to the invalid and his carers.

'Good evening Georgina.'

Pushing back her hair, Georgina looks up at Mulligan. His arm lies around the shoulder of the girl, the girl who sat next to Jeremy during the concert. Bewildered, she returns to watch over Richard.

'Hallo Tony,' this without looking at him further.

'Anything I can do to help? Looks as though he's in good hands. I'm sure he'll be fine.'

Georgina shakes her head in response as she absently wonders why Jeremy was with this girl who now apparently belongs with Mulligan. She feels the ominous presence of Mark who stands beside her but apart.

Richard becomes aware of his adversary's presence and twists his head to see Mulligan standing with his PA. Time is short and he gets straight to the point.

'Who is she, Tony?' Richard's voice is low and strained.

'Rich, I won't ask how you're doing. I can see you're not good.' Mulligan steps away from the girl and appraises her up and down. 'Who is she? Well, why don't I introduce you properly, in case you're not well enough for the round-up meeting tomorrow? This is Penny, Melanie's daughter. Thought you'd be curious to see how she turned out.'

Richard stares at the girl who returns a triumphant look.

'What the hell's going on here?' Georgina places herself between her husband and the two interlopers. She is unnerved by the mention of Melanie. Her earlier fears surface again. 'Tony, I think you should leave. Can't you see that Richard is seriously ill?'

'Yes, she's right,' adds Jeremy. 'You should leave Dad alone and go, right now, both of you.' He glares at the girl who sat beside him throughout the Mahler and now suspects their relationship.

Penny addresses Jeremy.

'What year were you born?'

'What the fuck has that to do with anything? Why are you bothering my Dad?'

She shrugs and smiles.

'Maybe you should ask 'Dad' that question.'

Mulligan smiles without warmth.

'So glad you're here too, Georgina. I thought you might be interested to meet Penny, too. You did meet Melanie didn't you? When you and Rich first met?'

Georgina shudders. Her breathing is tight. Of course she knew that her husband was involved with Melanie before they met. Now, crowding in on that memory is the face of this girl and the resemblance she spotted earlier across the hall, that look of Tricia, Richard's sister.

She tries to suppress rising panic and looks questioningly at Richard, seeking something to deny her suspicion, but his eyes are fixed on the girl. *Oh no. Please, God, no. She's his child. Richard's child. His daughter.*

'But you've been very ill, in a wheelchair ...' Richard's voice tails off. 'I came to see you once ...'

'Wonderful what the doctors can do these days, eh, Penny?' Mulligan answers for her. The girl is dismayed. When did he come to see her? How old was she? Where? Did her mother know and hide it from her?

The words she planned to say to her father desert her.

Jeremy grabs wildly at Mulligan's arm. He sees distress in his father's face, horror in the eyes of his mother. Whatever lies behind their fear, all he comprehends is that this man is bad, bad for his father, bad for his mother, for them all.

The people tending Richard call for calm, for everyone to leave. Mark moves in purposefully.

'You heard what my brother said. Just go, you aren't wanted here,' he hisses as he goes to drag Mulligan up the steps and away. No longer a young man, Mulligan is nonetheless strong and pushes back. Mark crashes into Jeremy who trips over a chair and plunges to the ground, little hurt other than his pride.

Benjamin has stood apart witnessing the drama. It is not his fight but he smells something very wrong. He parks his instrument and grabs Mulligan.

'Look mate, what don't you understand? Richard's sick and you're making things worse.'

The girl thrusts her face close to the violinist and says: 'Take your hands off of him.'

Benjamin shoves Mulligan away and whispers at the girl: 'Piss off, whoever you are.' He grabs her shoulders and twists her away.

She clutches at him and locks onto his left hand.

The acoustics of the concert hall convey the sound of not only the softest triangle beat, the crinkliest sweet wrapper, but also the snap of a finger joint.

Benjamin's scream of pain echoes up to the high empty seats of the Grand Tier. Momentarily everyone stops and looks.

Two paramedics arrive with large bags of equipment and confer with the first-aider and the concert-going doctor before taking over.

'Georgina,' Richard calls breathlessly. She leans over her husband as the paramedics attend to him.

'I'm sorry. It's all such a mess. Penny … I didn't want to hurt you ...' He loses consciousness. Georgina starts to weep soundlessly.

'That's it folks, everyone out. Now,' calls the paramedic. 'That includes you too madam.' The hall's first-aider shepherds everyone away from the seats and up into the corridor beyond.

Mulligan and the girl are already on their way. As they turn the final corner, she looks back over her shoulder and sees the woman standing in the archway. Her half-brother leans against the wall for support, head thrown back, eyes tightly clenched. The first-aider helps the trembling, grey-faced musician.

'Come on Penny, back to the hotel. Time for a nightcap I think.'

The girl looks back at her father, her family. There is no option. She sweeps out behind him but feels no triumph.

Georgina feels cold and her whole body aches. She pulls her cardigan close. She looks over to Benjamin who is visibly in pain. *What did that girl do to you?* The snap of the bone is lodged for ever in her mind. *That's his fingering hand.* She looks down onto the hunched backs in garish yellow, both working to save her husband. *Dear God, what will become of us all?*

Through her desolation, Georgina turns to face her two sons but cannot communicate. They observe her. There is no coming together now, nor will there ever be. Each of them is alone among others.

Richard is dying.

Georgina watches Richard carried past her towards the waiting ambulance. Someone offers to drive her to the hospital and she accepts. She collects her bag and walks out of the concert hall.

THE END

ABOUT THE AUTHOR

Jean Renwick discovered classical music later in life and although not a musician, she appreciates how music can echo and influence our mood. Writing this, her first novel, started after retirement and three years at university studying Art History. Her inspiration came from many rewarding hours spent listening to her favourite symphony orchestra when her mind would wander free.

Each chapter was written while listening to the relevant movement of Mahler's Fifth Symphony played by the Berlin Philharmonic under the baton of Sir Simon Rattle. None of the characters in this novel is based on real people.

Printed in Great Britain
by Amazon